CHASING
the DREAM

MONTANA SKIES
Book 3

CHASING
the DREAM

PAIGE LEE
ELLISTON

Revell
Grand Rapids, Michigan

© 2006 by Paige Lee Elliston

Published by Fleming H. Revell
a division of Baker Publishing Group
P.O. Box 6287, Grand Rapids, MI 49516-6287

Printed in the United States of America

Library of Congress Cataloging-in-Publication Data
Elliston, Paige Lee, 1943–
    Chasing the dream / Paige Lee Elliston.
        p.   cm. — (Montana skies ; bk. 3)
    ISBN 10: 0-8007-5941-9 (pbk.)
    ISBN 978-0-8007-5941-4 (pbk.)
    1. Women journalists—Fiction. 2. Montana—Fiction. I. Title. II. Series: El-liston, Paige Lee, 1943– Montana skies ; bk. 3.
PS3605.L4755C475 2006
813′.6—dc22   2006011753

This one is for Jaye Chambery,
who made all the difference.

1

"Big Sky Country, my foot," Amy Hawkins grumbled as she watched sheets of rain skitter across the vast expanse of burgeoning grass that was her front lawn. When the lawn—the full two acres of it, including the front and the back—went in almost three weeks ago, the rain had started. At first, it was gentle and nurturing, and Amy had welcomed it. Now, it seemed like the sort of deluge Noah faced, and the uniform drab gray of sodden day after sodden day was depressing. This certainly wasn't the glorious Montana weather she had expected.

Amy stepped back from the window, and her foot found a home on the spike tail of Nutsy, the kitten she'd adopted a month before. Nutsy reacted as cats—regardless of age—do: he yowled with a wail that was far too big and loud for his diminutive body, arched his back, hissed, and dashed off to cower under the couch, his favorite fortress against the often cruel and confusing world.

A hissing streak of chain lightning flickered outside, followed immediately by a sharp crack like the report of a gun, which preceded the now-familiar hollow boom of thunder.

Amy walked across her living room and stood gazing out of the picture window into her front yard. The house smelled new, as did the furniture, and the fine scent of the wall-to-wall carpeting was still strong. She smiled at the aroma.

Amy, with an architect friend, had designed the house. It was a modest-sized two bedroom, one-and-a-half bath, but seemed like a luxury cottage to Amy after living the last few years in a small and terribly overpriced New York City apartment. When she wasn't on the road, working for one writer or another, that is. Her parents' mansion in Connecticut, where she had spent her childhood and pre-college life, had always seemed to Amy like a cruise ship run aground—a look and a feeling she strived to avoid in her new home.

Starting a new life is a great concept, Amy thought. *But is it possible at age thirty-five?* She grinned. *It sure is—and I'm doing it.* A geographical change didn't eliminate or even alter the baggage of the past. All of that stayed solidly in place, she knew. But just because the weight existed in the past didn't mean it had to be hefted and carried in the present. *Being an itinerant book editor and all that went with it was then—this is now.*

Confined too long by the weather to sit comfortably, Amy paced through her home like a lioness in a cage. She stopped at the sliding doors off the kitchen and looked at her reflection in the glass. Her hair, brunette and shoulder length, framed a finely sculpted face—high cheekbones, a delicate nose, and a generous, smiling mouth. Her eyes, a rich, liquid brown, were perhaps Amy's best and certainly most striking feature. Tall for a woman at five-foot-ten, Amy had decided early on not to give in to the tall girl stoop, the mildly hunched stance many taller girls opted for in order to appear shorter. That, Amy thought, made as much sense as a man calling attention to his baldness by wearing a cheap toupee.

Amy's laptop was on the kitchen table, where it had rested since yesterday afternoon. As an editor now branching out into the world of writing fiction, she had few demands on her time other than those she imposed on herself. That was at least partially what the Montana move was all about—a place to see if the novel she'd fantasized about for years could actually turn into anything that might snare the reading public's attention.

The problem with all that, Amy admitted, was writer's block—a crippling state of mind that steps on creativity, joy in writing, and progress on a project. Amy had never actually believed in writer's block in the past. She'd attributed it to either fatigue or simple laziness on the part of the writer. Now, she realized, it was neither. It was a very real and quite frightening problem with which she now wrestled on a daily basis. Writer's block was doing a fine job of robbing her of sleep and casting shadows of self-doubt into her days. "I can beat this" had become a mantra-like affirmation, but it often felt to her like whistling in the cemetery, a weak attempt to push away her fear.

Up until now, everything for her career change had clicked into place like the movement of a fine watch. Her reputation as an editor—and three bestsellers she'd worked on, two of which were made into major box-office hits—had gotten her a famous and very effective literary agent. Inheriting a significant amount of money from an obscure great-aunt she had met a grand total of two times as a preteen had made the move and the home possible. The money, however, was finite, and Amy had quickly learned that anything and everything having to do with building and furnishing a new home was astoundingly expensive. The advance on her novel her agent had been able to negotiate had been sizable—not in the six-figure range heavyweights such as King and Updike garnered, but a good sum nevertheless. Now, though, her bank balance had dwindled to subsistence money, and the numbers kept her awake late at night. Her novel, she knew, could save her. But the way it was going . . . Amy shuddered.

A gust of wind slapped the side of the house. Amy smiled—not a window rattled. The rain continued to beat down, sweeping in gray sheets across her property and onto that of Jake Winter, her horse-farmer neighbor. *There's a strange one*, Amy thought. *Perfectly content to ride around on his quarter horses and grow his thousand or so acres of hay and live alone, except for the cowboys who work for him. Takes all kinds . . .*

Jake had ridden over when the construction people were digging Amy's basement and beginning her landscaping and introduced himself. He was a good-looking guy, maybe a couple of years older than her, who was dressed in a faded denim jacket, jeans, and boots. His eyes were a pale blue, which in some faces could have appeared weak or submissive. The depth of Jake's tan and the strong line of his jaw made his eyes look open, friendly, almost mischievous, as if only he knew the coming punch line of a joke.

"What are those fellows doing there?" Jake asked, pointing at a small backhoe that was digging a doghouse-size pit every dozen feet or so and following a line of white twine attached to short metal rods stuck into the ground.

"I have a load of bushes coming in the next couple of days," Amy said. "They're going to follow the driveway up to the house."

"The bushes are already mature?" Jake asked. "Most folks buy seedlings and . . ."

"Patience isn't my strongest virtue." Amy smiled.

He met her smile with his own. "I can't say it's mine, either."

Jake let his eyes roam over Amy's property. "Fine piece of land. I didn't even know ol' man Woerner was selling it until I saw you up here walking around with the Realtor from town." He shook his head. "Mr. Woerner never much cared for me since my friends and I tossed a string of cherry bombs into his privy one Halloween night a bunch of years ago."

"I hope there was no one in it."

"No, there wasn't," Jake said. "I'll admit that it made a bit of a mess, though. Anyway, that's probably why Woerner didn't come to me when he wanted to sell."

"Would you have bought this parcel?" Amy asked.

"Well . . . probably. Yeah. I guess there's no such thing as owning too much land."

Jake's horse snorted, and Jake turned to the animal, whose reins he held loosely in his left hand. "I'd better get this boy home," he said. "I have chores waiting." He stepped into a stirrup and swung easily into his Western saddle. "Do you ride, Amy?"

"Not since a pony ride on my sixth birthday," Amy said.

Jake grinned. "I have an ol' mare I can put you on. If you like, we can go out on horseback, and I can show you around a bit. There're Indian burial grounds not far from here that not many know about. Maybe you'd like to see them."

"I'd love to, Jake. Thanks."

Jake nodded. "Good, then. See you soon." He turned his horse away from Amy and loped off toward his own land, the horse's hooves thunking heavily on the soil and steel shoes tossing an occasional divot into the air behind them.

The sound of a vehicle entering her driveway brought Amy back to the present. Through the sheets of rain and mist at her window, she watched a red Dodge pickup wend its way toward the house. She tugged the business card out of her jeans pocket and read it once again: "Julie Pulver, Reporter" it stated, with the words superimposed over the American eagle logo of the *Coldwater News-Express*. Amy scurried to the front door and opened it wide. "Come on in," she called. "Hurry—you'll get soaked!"

The reporter had called two days before to request an interview. Amy had been perplexed then—and still was now—about why *News-Express* readers would have any interest in her. But, she thought, such a piece could serve as an introduction to her new neighbors and her new town.

Julie had stopped her truck in front of the main entrance to the house and now hefted herself onto the passenger bucket seat to avoid part of the frantic rush through the driving rain. She hustled out of the truck, slammed the door, and rushed up the steps.

Amy stepped aside, smiling. "Welcome, Julie. I'm Amy Hawkins. Here, let me take your coat. Isn't this rain something?"

"It sure is." Julie smiled. "What the farmers around here call a 'frog choker.'"

Amy looked at her visitor. Even the short rush from her vehicle to the house had left the woman's hair sopping wet and her denim jacket dripping. "I'll get a towel for your hair," she said. "Go on into the living room by the fireplace."

Amy selected her thickest, most absorbent towel from her linen closet, handed it to Julie, and then watched as the reporter stood in front of the fire, unself-consciously drying her hair. *All these Montana women look so healthy*, Amy thought. *So natural. Look at her—no fat anywhere, the face of a movie star, and she makes her jeans, boots, and shirt look designer-made for her.*

"Coffee?" Amy asked. "Or tea or Diet Pepsi?"

"Coffee sounds great," Julie said. "Black, please."

When Amy returned to the living room with two cups of coffee on a small Japanese-style tray, Julie had settled into a love seat adjacent to the fireplace, pen in hand, yellow legal pad on her lap. Amy sat in a matching love seat on the other side of the fire.

13

Julie looked around the living room appreciatively. "This is a fantastic home," she said. "It's really charming."

"Thanks. It's kind of eclectic, I guess. It's a culmination of things and features I've always wanted in a house—lots of glass, so there's lots of light, open rooms, wood everywhere, no chrome, and none of that sterile, hard-edged furniture."

Julie nodded. "Why Coldwater, Amy?"

The question caught Amy off guard. She'd expected more house questions: number of square feet, how many bedrooms and bathrooms, and the thinly veiled digging to determine what the place cost. "Well . . . I guess a number of reasons. I love the state, for one thing. I've spent time here—the Billings area, actually—with a husband and wife team of mystery writers. I've never really been comfortable in cities. I had a Realtor looking for land for me, and this piece came up for sale, and here I am."

"But why Coldwater in particular?"

"It was kind of strange about Coldwater. After I finished editing the Mountain Man series of books, I rented an SUV and kind of wandered through the state. I was simply driving and gawking, with no destination—not even a daily plan—in mind. I came to Coldwater, and I stopped at the bakery on Main Street and stood on the sidewalk eating a donut and felt the texture of the town and fell in love with it."

"Texture? What do you mean by that?"

Amy reflected for a moment. "You know how places— towns, cities, even homes—have a particular feel to them? Whether they're welcoming or unwelcoming? But sometimes a place simply feels good and right. That's how Coldwater felt to me that day." After a heartbeat, she added, "It still does."

Julie's smile was warm. "I know what you mean about certain places. I was never so safe and loved and warm as I was in my grandmother's kitchen. It had a feel all of its own."

"Exactly."

The reporter changed gears. "I've seen some of your work, Amy. It's impressive. The *Dancing Days—Crying Nights* book Lucas Reynolds dedicated to you was great."

Again, Julie's words were honest, without hype.

"Thanks. Lucas was great to work with. But now, instead of editing, I'm writing a novel, and it's my first venture into fiction." She smiled. "I think a lot of editors think of themselves as undiscovered novelists—or screenwriters. I know it's a cliché. But still, the things I've seen and the people I've talked to and have gotten to know give me all kinds of plots and themes and characters."

"I know what you mean," Julie agreed. "I'm an aspiring novelist myself. I've been working on mine for over a year."

Amy grinned. "Well—a fellow dreamer! We'll have to compare notes on writing fiction."

"That'd be fun. Let's do it soon." Julie thought for a moment before going on. "I suspect books have been a major part of your life since you were a child. Am I right?"

"You sure are. My mom and dad always had books around—they were great readers, and my dad read to me every night at bedtime. I picked up the love of reading from them and . . . well . . . here I am."

"Tell me a little about your childhood, Amy."

"I'm afraid there's nothing very exciting about it." Amy laughed. "I guess I was a typical middle-class American girl. I was a good student, involved in clubs and church groups, in love with various grungy rock stars, all that. When I was fifteen I went through a phase of wearing thrift store clothes and those army boot clodhoppers—it drove my parents nuts."

They laughed together. "Didn't we all," Julie said. "Maybe driving our parents nuts was part of it, no?"

"Sure. Harmless rebellion type of thing. And it was fun, too. Oh—one other thing I remember about that—the kids I hung out with all carried their books and things in brown paper sacks instead of the fancy backpacks that were the style then."

Julie pretended to be greatly impressed. "Wow! You and your pals really struck a blow against materialism and conformity!"

Again, they laughed easily and comfortably together. "When did you start writing?" Julie asked.

"I can't remember not writing, actually. I wrote stories for my parents, and I recall writing plays and bribing my friends with candy to act out the various roles. I've always loved the process of turning a piece of blank paper into a word picture of life and action and love and have others see that picture."

"When did you begin editing?"

"In high school. It came easily to me—I could see almost intuitively what the writer was after, what he or she was trying to say, and I had the words to make those concepts clearer. I found that I loved editing almost as much as writing."

"And in college?"

"I got lucky. I won an academic scholarship and became a junior editor on the campus literary magazine. I really liked that work, and the writers I edited seemed pleased with what I did with their stuff. In my junior year, I was made the managing editor, and I loved it. I had tons of stories and articles to edit, and I worked with the junior editors, and . . ." She smiled deprecatingly. "I'm rattling on about myself too much."

"Not at all. I'm here to learn about you," Julie answered.

"Let me ask this," Amy said. "Why will your readers care about me? I'm not being self-effacing, but there are tons of struggling writers around. I'm not a name or a celebrity or anything close to it. Book editing fame lasts about as long as it takes to step in a puddle during a rainstorm."

"At least a few reasons," Julie answered, making eye contact with Amy. "You're single, attractive, and new here." She grinned then. "Maybe *new* is the operative word, but the single and attractive don't hurt in terms of reader interest. Neither does the fact that you're a full-time writer. That's a glamour profession in my readers' eyes."

Amy laughed at the reporter's candor. "You get right to the point, don't you?" She thought about what Julie had said for a moment. "A glamour profession? Only if you consider grinding away all day, every day, scrounging for the right word, the perfect line of dialogue, the most vivid character. I don't see much glamour in that. Don't get me wrong. I love the entire process of writing fiction, but it's work, just like any other job." She smiled, adding another thought. "And except for the biggies who write the bestsellers, the pay is awful."

Julie scratched a few words on her pad. "No one gets rich reporting for a small newspaper either," she observed. "Still, we do it, and it's a paycheck every two weeks. That's something you don't have right now, right?"

"Right. I saved some money, and I got an inheritance from a relative I hardly knew a few years ago, but the house cost more than I estimated. Actually, everything—furniture, carpet, all that—cost more than I estimated. So it's pretty important that my novel catch on and sell well."

Julie smiled. "Dare I say 'movie contract' or 'TV series'?"

Amy laughed. "Only in my dreams."

Thunder boomed, and both women instinctively looked over at the picture window. A silence followed, but it wasn't an uneasy one.

Amy glanced at Julie's left hand. "I see you're married," she said, swinging the conversation away from herself.

"About a year ago—a great guy. You'll have to meet Danny. He's a veterinarian. You've probably seen his van around."

"He's the guy with that big collie, right? I saw him at the coffee shop in town a couple of times."

"Right—Drago's Café is kind of the meeting place of

Coldwater. Everyone goes there for the coffee—and for the gossip."

"Well, I'm looking forward to meeting Danny."

"What about you, Amy? Is there a guy in your life?"

She shook her head. "I've never married. I guess I just didn't have time. I think someday I'll meet a handsome prince on a white charger, but I'm not actively looking for him. Whatever happens, happens."

"What about when your novel's finished? Where to then?"

"I really am planning on permanence. I want to fit in here, become a part of the people I respect and like so much. I've done enough traveling and I've lived out of enough suitcases to last me for the rest of my life."

Julie rose. "I'm sure you'll fit just fine, Amy. This is a good place to live. I guess you already know that, or you wouldn't be here." She held out her hand.

Amy took Julie's hand in a firm handshake. "Please stop by or call whenever you care to," Amy said. "I'd like it a lot if you did."

"I will," Julie promised. "And you do the same. I'd love for you to meet Danny and my friend Maggie Lane and her husband, Ian, our minister."

Amy watched as Julie dashed to her truck through the rain, started the engine, and drove down the driveway to the road. She looked at the business card Julie had given her. On the back, Julie had written her home telephone number, her husband's veterinary clinic number, and her cell phone listing. Amy folded the card carefully and put it in her shirt pocket.

She turned from the door after shutting it, shivering a bit from the damp breeze that had invaded her home as Julie left. The rain continued its monotonous assault, and a sharp burst of thunder startled her. She hadn't seen the lightning this time, but the blast was terribly loud and immediate—not the muted thunder she'd become accustomed to. It was followed by a strange sensation that stopped her from taking a step—a sort of barely discernible trembling under her feet. The silence after the thunder seemed slightly different too. Along with the vibration, Amy heard—or perhaps felt more than heard—a very soft drumming, almost like the vibration of a nearby train in a city.

"What in the world . . . ?" Amy mumbled to herself as she walked to the kitchen and looked out the window over the sink.

A pair of large, chestnut brown eyes stared back at her through the rain-streaked glass. Amy yelped and leaped back. The horse reacted similarly, snuffing and rearing. The animal wheeled and bolted, and the thrumming sensation became more pronounced as Amy stepped back to the window.

Twenty or so quarter horses in headlong flight from something or other churned past the rear of Amy's home, their shod hooves sinking inches into the soupy, water-logged soil, punching sloppy holes with each impact, tearing tender young grass away from its precarious hold and flinging it aside in their wakes.

Amy raced back to the picture window facing the driveway, where her bushes had been lovingly planted and where the grass had barely taken hold. A flood of moving color—bay, black, chestnut, dapple-gray, white—washed over the grounds. As she watched, horrified, a pair of running mares collided, and one went down on her side on the sodden earth. Her legs flailing, she skidded over one of Amy's bushes, flattening it before she scrambled to her feet. A thump from the rear of the house drew Amy back to the kitchen. She ran to the window, and once again an equine face peered, wide-eyed, back at her.

"Shoo!" Amy yelled. The horse skittered away from the window as another slid and skidded against the back of the house.

Amy yanked the telephone from the wall and glared at the crumpled business card Jake had given her and that she'd carried in a back pocket of her jeans until her house was built. Tacking it to her corkboard had been one of the first moving-in things she'd done. She punched in the numbers with a trembling finger.

"This is Jake," the man's voice answered, his tone slow and welcoming. "I'm sorry I wasn't here to talk with you, but if you'll leave your name and number, I'll get right back to you as soon as—"

She slammed the receiver back onto the wall mount. There was another thud as a horse banged into her house. "That does it!" she grumbled, grabbing a jacket from the small kitchen closet. She dashed into the attached garage, climbed into her Jeep Cherokee, and thumbed the electronic garage door opener. As the door lifted she cranked the

Jeep's engine to life. Two horses stood in the driveway just beyond the garage. Amy laid on the horn, and the animals hustled out of her way. She backed down the driveway and scanned the damage to her landscaping. The lawn looked like it had been strafed by dozens of enemy aircraft, the bare spots opened by hooves pocking its surface. A chestnut horse was casually grazing on one of her bushes and eyeing the Jeep as it approached. Amy blasted the horn again, and the horse reluctantly moved away, a short branch dangling casually from its mouth and bobbing between the animal's lips as it chewed.

Amy raced down the rest of her driveway and spun her tires in a full-throttle leap toward Jake's home. She careened up his driveway and skidded to a shuddering stop outside the main barn, an impossibly long and wide structure Amy had been told contained an indoor riding arena, Jake's rodeo operation offices, stalls for animals, and hay and grain storage areas. As she opened the door of her Jeep, the drumming of the rain on the metal of the barn was almost deafening. A cowhand seated on a bale of straw under a roof overhang at the side of the building worked quite industriously with a large, curved, leather-sewing needle, repairing a bridle. The fellow was thin, and he was wearing jeans, a work shirt with the sleeves rolled to midarm, rundown Western boots, and a Stetson that looked older than Methuselah's grandmother. She exited her car, slammed the door, and sprinted to the cowboy's side.

"I need to see Mr. Winter," she said. "Is he around?"

The man's face was wrinkled from decades in the elements, but the crinkles around his startlingly blue eyes were friendly, put there by laughter. "Jake's inside with a buyer," he said. "Just go on in."

"Well, look—there's a herd of his horses tearing up my yard, and I need them off my property," Amy said. "Can you ..."

"You'd best see Jake about that," the cowhand said. "Like I say, jus' go on in the door here an' follow the aisle to the big ring in the middle. Jake'll be there."

Amy glared for a moment and then decided the man was right—she needed to speak directly with Mr. Winter. She tugged open the door and stepped inside the building. Her first surprise was how quiet it was inside. She'd expected a machine gun–like racket from the rain assaulting the metal sides and roof of the structure. She glanced upward and saw that insulation ran between the joists many feet above her head, muffling the impact of the storm.

She looked down a long, fluorescent-lighted aisle that seemed to stretch to the next horizon. There were doors off it, just as there'd be in an office building. The floor, however, was a gritty, sandy-colored substance—not quite dirt but not far from it, either. The air was richly fragrant with the scent of cut hay, fresh soil, and animals. It reminded her of childhood summers spent at various youth camps. It was a good, clean, evocative aroma that generated quick images of sunshine and expanses of fenced land and small lakes and laughing kids in camp T-shirts.

Amy started down the aisle, not quite comfortable in the cathedral-like silence, and peeked in whichever doors happened to be open. One she passed was equipped with three desks, each with a computer monitor on it, a series of beige filing cabinets, a large copier, a fax machine on a counter, and boxes of what appeared to be brochures and catalogs stacked neatly against one wall. The office had a shiny oak floor, Amy noticed. As she stood in the doorway, a telephone buzzed with businesslike authority. A machine answered with an abrupt click in the midst of the second buzz, but Amy couldn't hear the outgoing message. A large sign on the rear wall told any visitor that he or she had entered J. W. Quarter Horses & Rodeo Stock, Inc. The printing was centered over a logo of a cowboy on a bucking bronco. Amy hustled on toward the center of the massive building, her shoes making quiet, shuffling sounds as she hurried along.

There was a door at the end of the aisle at a point Amy figured was halfway into the building. As she came closer to it she felt the thrumming of hooves lightly through her soles. She opened the door and passed through. Now she was in an arena that seemed as broad and as deep as a baseball field, except that it lacked the seating. Set in the center of the expanse was a movable corral made of pipes. Inside the corral were ten or so horses that moved about nervously, as if they didn't care to be there.

Jake Winter, his back to her, stood with a boot on the lowest rail of the enclosure. Next to him a shorter, slighter man with long, raven black hair stood in an almost mirror image of Jake's stance.

Amy smiled. *It seems like all cowboys stand like that*, she thought. *They're like policemen, in a sense—they can always be*

24

picked out of a crowd. It wasn't their clothing, either. These Montana cowboys could never be mistaken for insurance salesmen or dentists or mail carriers. There was something about these guys—the way they stood, the way they moved, the way they used their bodies. Even in the diner in Coldwater, Amy could pick out the cowboys just by watching them walk through the door and step up to the counter.

Neither of the two noticed Amy coming up behind them. The conversation they were involved in seemed deep, important to both of them. Although she couldn't see their faces, Amy realized that their eyes were focused on the horses in front of them. She stopped a few yards away, not wanting to intrude quite yet.

Jake's words—at least most of them—reached her. "I'd go with the chestnut, Juan. You give him the time he needs, and you'll be roping in the Calgary finals next season."

The other man's voice was lower and a bit hesitant. "The chestnut is a fine horse."

"Yep. He is that."

"I don' have that much money, Jake."

Jake shook his head. "Look here; you're one of the best calf ropers I've ever seen. You take that chestnut out there and work him, and you'll be making good money at every rodeo you hit. Give me a down payment and the rest on installments."

Juan nodded his head and turned to face Jake. "You know that my word, it is good."

"'Course it is," Jake huffed impatiently. "I got things to do, my friend. Bring your trailer around the back, and Wes or one of the other boys will help you load the horse. It's a done deal. Like I said, I got things to do."

Juan stood flat-footed, hands at his sides, shaking his head very slightly, as if dazed. Jake turned to him and held out his right hand. Juan took it slowly and shook it formally, as if sealing a deal—which he was.

That sure isn't the way we do business in publishing, Amy mused. She cleared her throat to get Jake's attention.

Jake, surprised at seeing her, smiled and stepped closer. "Amy, good to see you. What's up?" His eyes teased her. "Looking for a good horse?"

"Uh, no, I'm not looking for a horse."

"So, then, to what do I owe the honor of your visit?"

"Well . . . a bunch of your horses got loose and ripped up my new lawn. They wrecked some of my bushes along the driveway too. I don't know how to get them off my property, and each time they move, they sink in and tear up grass. It's a real mess."

"Whoa—I'm sorry, Amy. Must be some of my mares got through the fence. I'll get the horses off your property right away—right now—but I'll have to wait until the ground dries a bit before I can have the area rolled for you." He looked her in the eye. "It'll look as good as new, I guarantee that. And I'll replace any shrubs and lawn they wrecked."

"Thank you. I appreciate that."

"I'll make sure the fence is good and tight and ratchet up the electricity going through it. That'll keep the mares where they belong. What probably happened is that lightning struck a fence post and shorted out the system. I'll back up that fence line so this won't happen again." Jake tugged a cell phone from his back pocket and flipped it open. "Why don't you go on home and I'll get a couple of men and be right over to shag those old girls off your lawn. OK?"

He turned away from Amy, then pushed the speed dial on his phone and began talking. "Billy," he said, "get whoever's there mounted up and meet me out front. Our mares must've busted through the east fence, and they're ripping up our neighbor's lawn. And hustle, Billy. This needs to be done right now."

Jake turned back to Amy. "If you can find your way out, I'll go through the back here, grab a horse, and get over to your place. OK?"

"Sure, Jake. I appreciate your attitude about all this."

"I'm just sorry it happened." He paused for a moment. "Maybe we can get together soon? Maybe go for that ride after the rain stops?"

"Okay. I'll look forward to it." Amy smiled.

Jake climbed over the enclosure, and Amy started back in the direction from which she'd come through the building. *Get together soon? You bet!*

A couple of men in slickers on horseback were already at her house as Amy pulled into her driveway. One whirled a loop of lariat over his head as his horse charged toward one of the intruders. The loop flashed out as accurate as a rifle shot and settled around the other horse's neck. The rider turned his mount and led the captured mare back toward the Winter pasture. The other rider herded a pair of horses in front of his own, whistling shrilly, goading them toward their home. Jake appeared on a big chestnut quarter horse as Amy pulled into her garage. She watched through the garage window as the men worked the loose horses.

Jake rode with an easy and unconscious grace that told of a lifetime in the saddle. He moved with the horse—almost as if he were part of the animal—and seemed to be conveying very few commands to his mount, even though the horse was turning and changing gaits quickly, heading off and directing a couple of the mares.

It didn't take more than ten minutes until Jake and one of the cowhands were cutting the last mare back into the pasture. Several men were stretching new wire between fence posts already, and the fence line was secure within moments of the last horse being chased home.

Amy looked over the lawn before going into her house. Without the horses and men the expanse was forlorn and quiet. It was a swampy mess of more mud-brown than grass-green, pocked with countless holes, deep skid marks, and scattered branches torn from the bushes.

She sighed and shivered a bit as she walked into her kitchen. It wasn't actually cold out, although July in Montana was reputed to be a whole lot hotter than the current temperature. Still, the bleak grayness of the rain carried its own chill.

Amy ground some coffee beans; the sound of the little machine seemed harsh and screechy in the quietude of her home. She poured the ground coffee into a filter she'd placed in her Mr. Coffee, added three cups of cold springwater, and watched the coffee brew. Good coffee chased chills and improved perspectives, she believed.

Amy poured a mugful and carried it to her kitchen table, setting it next to her laptop. She sat, sipped, and clicked on the computer. It made its strange little whirring sounds, and in moments the page where she'd left off the night before appeared on the screen, the letters crisp and sharp against the white of the screen.

I started yesterday on this page, wrote four pages, deleted each of them, and ended up here again. Swell progress.

Amy had begun *The Longest Years*, a fictional chronicle of a large farm family during the Great Depression, almost a year ago. The characters, Amy was certain, were strong and believable, the plot solidly based on actual history, and the drama intense without being overpowering. Categorized as "romance/history/action-adventure," *The Longest Years* seemed to have the elements that fiction readers sought in the books they purchased or borrowed from libraries.

The story and the time period were close to Amy's heart. In college, her roommate, a girl from Oklahoma, had shared with her the diaries of her great-grandmother, who'd lived through the Depression years. Amy had been captivated immediately by the sheer courage and tenacity of the struggling, dozen-member family, and enchanted by their closeness. Hannah—the great-grandmother—possessed an indomitable and unshakable faith in the Lord, and her sense of humor never failed her. The protagonist in Amy's novel, renamed Sarah, had a quiet strength that carried the family—and the book—through the most desperate of times and situations.

What was wrong, then? Amy simply didn't know. Her novel had stalled at page 150 and showed no good signs of starting up again.

She sighed and leaned back in her chair, closing her eyes. She pictured Sarah and her family in her mind, sitting at their kitchen table, passing around jackrabbit stew and potatoes from the garden. Sarah and Calvin, Sarah's husband, were talking, their faces appearing strained and serious. The ten children were eating, talking, laughing—paying no attention to their parents. Amy could almost hear the conversation between Sarah and Cal. *Let it flow . . . let it come . . . listen to them . . .*

A cold, wet nub pressed against Amy's cheek. A half moment later a weight dropped into her lap. The weight mewed. Amy opened her eyes. Nutsy stared back at her, not at all abashed at having fallen off the laptop on the table and into Amy's lap. In fact, his demeanor indicated that he'd done it on purpose and that there'd been no uncatlike clumsiness involved.

Amy began to scratch lazily between the kitten's ears. His motor kicked in immediately, and to Amy the purring sound seemed louder than a kitten could logically produce. Nutsy's tongue on the underside of Amy's wrist felt like wet sandpaper.

She looked at the screen of her laptop where the line "m[kluy6tom32hg" appeared, establishing the fact that the cat had stood for a moment on the keyboard before leaning forward to Amy's face. She looked more closely at the line of characters and numbers.

How had "Tom" crept in there? The letters weren't close together on the keyboard—*O* and *M* were separated by a row of other letters, and the *T* was on the left half of the keyboard. *Back paw and front paw?*

It wasn't at all difficult to bring Tom Davis to mind. Amy saw him clearly—his six-foot-two frame, his grin, the warm depths of his keen brown eyes. He'd been a basketball star in high school and college—the college he'd attended on a full athletic scholarship, even though the tuition would have been pocket change for his very wealthy parents.

Tom was the kid with the new Porsche, the charming and handsome guy the girls mooned over, the playmaker on any team he joined. He'd been strangely free of the arrogance most high school sports heroes developed, and if he was aware of the girls who flocked around him, he didn't show it. He and Amy had begun dating in their senior year. No one—Amy included—really expected the high school crush to last beyond a few months of college when the couple was separated by hundreds of miles.

It *had* lasted, at least until Tom began medical school. There, his basketball skills meant nothing, and for the first time in his academic career, he had to apply himself with every bit of strength he possessed to even stay parallel with his classmates. He maintained decent but not spectacular grades.

Something had to give. The weekend visits ended. Amy

was devoting the majority of her time to her first reporting job, and Tom was married to *Gray's Anatomy*.

The telephone calls became less frequent and then stopped altogether. Tom began keeping company with a classmate, a woman from Indonesia who was a top student. Together they spent most of their time studying. Amy began dating a musician she'd been sent to review and interview.

It wasn't that Amy and Tom's love had died; it simply had been overwhelmed by the life choices they made.

When Tom began his surgical residency at Harbor Hill Hospital in their hometown, Amy was freelancing articles to local and national magazines. They'd bumped into one another—literally—at a grocery store on the main street of Harbor Hill. Amy had been holding up a honeydew melon, eyeing it critically for ripeness, when a shopping cart struck her sharply in the hip. The melon had launched itself and thudded heavily to the floor, cracking the length of one side. Amy spun around to see who the clumsy oaf was who'd banged into her.

"I'm so sorry," Tom said apologetically. "This cart has a mind of its own—it turns whenever it wants to, without warning. I can't . . . Amy? Amy Hawkins?"

Amy couldn't answer at first. Emotions flooded over her, frighteningly strong, stealing her voice as she stared at Tom Davis. Finally, she managed, "Tom—it's good to see you."

They looked into each other's eyes for a long moment, neither speaking, each barely breathing, totally unaware of passing shoppers and the grating announcements and muzak that flowed from the store's speakers. Then they'd gone out to a coffee shop to catch up, each leaving a half-full shopping cart in the aisle. Two nights later they'd gone to dinner. The next weekend found them on Tom's sailboat on both Saturday and Sunday.

It was a whirlwind—and yet it wasn't. It was as if they'd severed the time that had passed—cut it from their lives and from their consciousness—and gone back to where they were before the weekend visits and telephone calls had ended.

"I don't really understand it," Tom said one night as they sat at a quiet table in a local restaurant. "How all my feelings could be rekindled so rapidly and completely. It doesn't make much sense—but there it is." He thought for a moment as he reached across the table and covered Amy's hand gently with his own. "Or maybe *rekindle* isn't the correct word, because maybe the fire never went out."

Amy nodded. "I know what you mean. We're very fortunate. Most people don't get a second chance with their first love. It just doesn't happen—but with us, it did."

It was an idyllic couple of years—a modern fairy tale. And then . . .

The impossible happened. Tom met a thoracic surgeon from Boston Hospital at a convention, and the romance of the century fell apart like a poorly assembled toy.

OK. Things like that happen. I'm over it. And now, I have a novel to worry about.

She was glad Nutsy was still in her lap. She picked up his warm, purring body and held him against her heart.

She had the dream again that night.

Everything in her kitchen looked the same: the windows, the sink, the appliances, Nutsy's water and food bowls, the kitchen table with her laptop sitting on it, screen up and ready. Nevertheless, the familiar room felt different—different in a disquieting way. Amy sat at the laptop and tapped the "on" switch. The keyboard flashed and the opening graphics appeared on the screen. The sounds of the computer were strange. Instead of the steady, electronic hum to which she was accustomed, the machine made a grinding sound, a metal-against-metal type of friction noise.

"It's nothing," Amy said aloud. "It's a little slow is all."

Her hands were slow to move to the position poised over the keyboard. Her fingers, her hands, both her forearms, were heavy, almost numb. She forced a smile through a growing sense of fear. "They'll be better soon. This will go away."

Although there was no specific idea in her mind, she pressed a key. Nothing happened. She pushed harder, and the key resisted her. She pecked at another key, and another. Nothing happened. The screen saver remained in place, the keys unyielding no matter how much pressure Amy exerted.

She shoved the laptop across the table; her tears made her vision shimmer. The grinding noise continued.

Amy's face was damp as she wrestled her way out of the dream. She awoke to find the sheets wrapped cocoon-like around her. She gasped for air as if she'd run a long distance, and her heart pounded crazily in her chest. Her hand trembled as she reached for her bedside lamp and clicked it to life. The light chased the darkness, but it seemed almost too brilliant, stinging her eyes for a few moments. She used the back of her hand to wipe away the tears.

"I can beat this," she said aloud. "I *will* beat this."

2

Two days later when Amy was awakened by Nutsy step-
ping on her head, something seemed very different in her
bedroom—not wrong necessarily but different. She smiled
when she realized what it was: pure, bright, warm sunshine
was streaming in through her window. Amy struggled out
from beneath her covers and walked the couple of steps
to the window. Then, she simply stood there in the broad
shaft of light, savoring the feel of it against her skin and
on her nightgown. Nutsy wove his way around and between her ankles, purring loudly, relishing the sensation
of sunlight on his coat.

Even the view of her lawn from the window couldn't
dampen Amy's mood. The grass still looked like a thousand
duffer golfers had been let loose on it and failed to replace
their multitudinous divots, but she ignored the damage
and let her eyes feast on the rapidly drying ground.

She hurried through her shower, dressed quickly, and
went downstairs to her kitchen. That room too was cheerful and welcoming, filled with brightness and warmth.
She opened the window over the sink, and the earthy,

fertile scent of Montana swept into her home, chasing the residual dampness and gloom as if it'd never existed. She hummed as she placed a fresh filter in her Mr. Coffee and ground enough beans for three large cups. The aroma of the coffee was in perfect partnership with the smells from outdoors—each tickled her senses delightfully. She added ice-cold water from the large Brita pitcher in her refrigerator and fed Nutsy while the coffee brewed.

This is the sort of day in which nothing can go wrong, Amy mused. She reached into a cupboard for her corn flakes and then stopped without taking down the box. *The end of the rain calls for a breakfast at Drago's Café, maybe even the cholesterol special: bacon, eggs, hash browns, a short stack of blueberry pancakes—with syrup.* She sat at her kitchen table with her first mug of coffee, her face still creased into a smile, just as it had been since her cat had awakened her. Her laptop was where she'd left it the night before. The computer hulked on the table like an electronic gargoyle, chiding her for not moving her novel forward.

"Later," she said aloud to the machine. "I have errands to run and a big breakfast to eat first." Amy laughed to herself, and her glee at her own silliness felt good to her. She wasn't one to speak to inanimate objects, but today doing so seemed perfectly sane and logical. She finished her coffee, put her mug in the dishwasher, checked Nutsy's water bowl, and grabbed her purse.

When she stepped out onto her front porch, she stopped abruptly, gaping at the black quarter horse that stood eyeing her lazily, its reins on the driveway surface. The old fellow she'd met outside the Winter barn strode around the corner of the garage.

"Mornin', Miss Amy," he said. "I never introduced myself the other day. My name's Wes—Wes Newton." He tipped his Stetson to her.

I don't think I've ever actually seen a man tip his hat to a lady before, she thought. "Morning, Wes. I'm pleased to meet you." After a moment, she added, "Can I help you with something?"

"Nome. Jake sent me over to kinda check on the ground—see how long it'd be before we can roll them holes for you. I'm thinkin' day after tomorrow if it doesn't rain again."

Nome? What does Alaska have to do with—wait. No, ma'am! Amy struggled against the laugh that rose in her throat. "I see," she said. "And you rode your horse over, I guess." *What a moronic remark*, she chided herself. *No, that's a big plastic lawn ornament Wes brought as a welcoming gift.*

Wes looked confused for a moment. "Why, 'course I did. A good cowhand don't walk nowhere he can ride to, and I never did learn to drive very good. So yeah, I rode over. Fact is, I ride just about everywhere I go." It seemed like a point of honor to the cowhand. Amy nodded.

"I'll be on my way, then," Wes said. He scooped up the reins and swung into his saddle with an easy agility that showed none of his age. "I'm around most all the time, Miss Amy. You feel free to call on me if you have trouble or need help with somethin', OK?"

"That's very kind of you, Wes. I'll keep you in mind. And I appreciate your coming over this morning."

Wes Newton tipped his hat again. Amy couldn't see him give a command to his mount, but apparently he did because the horse swung around and trotted down the driveway. Amy watched him for a long moment. His shoulders—his upper body—didn't move the least bit. It was as if he was welded to the seat of the saddle.

Amy backed her Jeep out of the double garage and performed a neat K-turn in order to drive forward down the driveway. Before entering the road she lowered her window and the one on the passenger side. The air was warm and fragrant with the scent of grass and soil and the slightest smell of clean, well-cared-for horses from Jake's pasture. It was like a perfume provided gratis by nature, free to anyone who appreciated it.

Julie Pulver's red pickup was parked in front of the café along with a half dozen or so other trucks and SUVs. Amy pulled in to the curb and shut off her engine. Her perfect day was continuing—it would be good to see Julie again. Julie seemed like a woman who could become a good friend, and Amy hoped that would happen.

A few heads turned to look Amy over as she walked into Drago's, but the majority of the small crowd was more interested in their breakfasts and their coffee. There was a pleasant, low-key buzz of conversation in the restaurant and an occasional burst of laughter. Julie sat facing the front in a booth across from another woman. Julie smiled and waved. "Amy—come on over and sit down and meet my friend Maggie."

The woman across from Julie turned to face Amy with a welcoming smile. She was very attractive, with even features and the scrubbed, wholesome look one saw in magazine advertisements for family vacation spots. Her eyes were coffee brown, and her hair was shoulder length and a chestnut brown. She extended her right hand to Amy.

"I'm Maggie Lane," she said. "Julie's told me about you and your home. I hope I'll get to see the inside some day. It's really striking from outside—just beautiful."

"Thanks," Amy said. "I wanted it to fit into the land rather than look like a boat beached on that little rise the house sits on. And I'd love to give you the grand tour anytime you want to take it. I mean it—stop by, OK?"

"You bet," Maggie said. "Sit down, Amy."

Julie shoved over to the wall, and Amy sat next to her, facing Maggie. "Julie said your husband is the minister here."

"Ian—yeah, he is. I'm sure you'll meet him soon. He's Coldwater's unofficial welcoming committee. Now that I think of it, I'll be with him when he comes to visit you. It's his policy not to call on single women by himself. You can show us both your house then."

"I'll look forward to it," Amy said. "Boy—I woke up salivating about a huge breakfast here in town, and I got to see Julie again and to meet you on top of it. And a minister who actually takes the time to call on new people? That's a new one to me."

"Ian believes in old-time ministering. I think you'll see that when you meet him." She paused for a moment, thinking. "You live next door to Jake Winter, right? Have you met him yet?"

"Sure. As a matter of fact, I was at his place a couple days ago. Some of his horses got through their fence and did a number on my lawn."

"Probably his broodmares in that east pasture, right?" Julie asked.

"Right—that's what Jake said, the east pasture. He seems like a great guy, and he's certainly a good neighbor. He's going to have his men roll my lawn."

"Jake is a great guy," Julie said.

Maggie nodded. "Most—maybe all—of the unmarried women around here think he's great too," she said, grinning. "When he was coaching the 4-H Horse Club, all the girls had crushes on him."

Amy laughed. "I guess I can see why." After a moment she asked, "Has he ever been married?"

"No," Julie answered. "He says he never had time. He's worked awful hard to build up his rodeo stock business, and, well, he couldn't even find time for casual dating, and certainly not for a relationship."

Maggie's cell phone disrupted the conversation. She dug it out of her purse, flipped it open, and said, "Hello, Maggie Lane." She listened for a long moment, and then the smile left her face. "OK, Ian," she said. "I'll be right home. We can go to the hospital together. I'm glad it's not more serious. Right. Bye." She returned the telephone to her purse.

"Annie Richards fell and broke her ankle," she said. "The ER doctor called Ian. We're going to stop in and see her." She looked at Amy. "Annie's ninety-two years old and gets confused at times. Ian's afraid she's giving the doctors a tough time. I'm so sorry, Amy—I was enjoying talking with you. But we'll see you when Ian and I visit."

"That'll be fun, and I'm looking forward to meeting Ian. We'll have more time to visit then. I'm sorry about Mrs. Richards."

"Me too," Julie said. "Tell Annie I said hello and sent my love."

"Will do." Maggie smiled. "See you soon, Amy." She turned and hurried from the café.

Ellen, a waitress at Drago's since the day it opened almost thirty years ago, appeared next to the booth. Julie introduced her to Amy.

"Good to meet you, Amy," Ellen said. "Welcome to Coldwater. You're going to like it here."

"I already do, Ellen. Nice to meet you too. I'm sure we'll be seeing a lot of one another."

"What can I bring you this morning?" Ellen asked, her pencil poised over her pad.

"I have this all planned." Amy smiled. "How about two eggs over easy, an order of bacon, a side of hash browns, and a short stack of blueberry pancakes—and coffee, please."

"Great," Ellen groaned. "You're just like Julie. You could eat a barrel of nails a day and never gain an ounce, right?"

"Well . . . weight's never been a problem . . ." Amy admitted.

Ellen shook her head in mock disgust. "If I had a breakfast like you just ordered, my rear end wouldn't fit on the seat of my lawn tractor." She smiled at the two women and walked off toward the kitchen, tearing the page with Amy's order from her pad.

The conversation went easily in the booth, interspersed with laughter. Amy's massive breakfast was perfect, and Julie lingered with her over coffee. They left Drago's together and said their good-byes on the sidewalk in front of the café. Amy climbed into her Jeep and sat for a moment as Julie drove off. She savored the moment, savored Coldwater, her new home.

Later that afternoon Amy sat at her kitchen table, laptop open and running in front of her. Nutsy slept on her lap. She wasn't a terribly rapid typist, so her fingers moved somewhat slowly but quite steadily over the keyboard.

On good days the images flowed from her brain and somehow translated themselves into words at her fingertips, and the pages filled with prose. It was, she thought, more of a semi-spiritual process than a physical or emotional one. And, she knew, some days were better than others. She read over the few paragraphs she'd written, sighed, and dragged the cursor backward over the lines, deleting them. The raucous jangle of her telephone interrupted her work. She took a deep breath and then answered the phone.

"Amy Hawkins."

"Hi, Amy. This is . . . uhhh . . . Jake." He paused for a moment. "Jake Winter."

Amy grinned. She'd recognized his voice after his first couple of words. "Hi, Jake. What's up?"

"Well . . . how are you, Amy?"

"I'm just fine," she answered, a bit puzzled. "I've had a really good day."

"I see."

He sees? OK, what is going on here?

The silence stretched almost to the breaking point. Amy could hear Jake breathing. Finally, he spoke again.

"I'm cooking up some burgers tonight. I thought maybe you'd want to come over for dinner." The words came more rapidly than she'd ever heard Jake speak. *This is like when boys would call me for dates when I was in high school! He's embarrassed to be calling me to ask me over. How sweet!*

"That sounds great, Jake. Suppose I make a big salad to bring along?"

"Sure. That'd be good."

"OK. What time?"

"Um—it's about twenty to four."

Amy bit back a giggle. "No, I mean what time should I come over?"

"Oh. Maybe 6:30?"

"OK. See you then."

"Amy?"

"Yes?"

"I don't much like talking on the telephone."

She had to bite back a giggle again. "No problem. It's not my favorite thing, either. See you at 6:30, Jake."

Amy's errands in Coldwater had included food shopping, and she had plenty of fresh salad components on hand. She fetched her large wooden bowl from a top cabinet and began washing leaves of lettuce. The fresh smell of the onions, the radishes, the lettuce itself, and the pair of handfuls of crumbled blue cheese she sprinkled over the salad made her mouth water in anticipation. She hadn't eaten since her breakfast in town.

Her mind returned to Jake's telephone call as she worked at the sink and counter. *I should take it as a real compliment that the guy is nervous talking to me, asking me to his place. There's a little-boy charm to him, whether he knows it or not. He's downright refreshing. This should be fun.*

She found herself humming and smiling as she stretched plastic wrap over the bowl and put the salad into her refrigerator. She looked at her kitchen clock: 4:45. *Plenty of time to take a leisurely shower and get dressed.* The dressing part would be easy: a pair of clean jeans, a Western blouse, and the boots she'd purchased earlier that month. As she took the blouse from her closet, her glance fell on the line of chic dresses and the several pairs of expensive, impracti-

46

cal shoes she'd arranged carefully when she moved in—and hadn't worn since that day. That too made her smile.

Jake's home appeared diminutive in comparison to the huge steel building that housed his business operations. Actually, it was a pleasant three-bedroom ranch, situated about fifty yards from the much-larger structure. There were, Amy noticed as she parked her Jeep behind Jake's Dodge pickup in the driveway, a series of outbuildings strewn about the property. The living quarters for the cow-hands—the bunkhouse—was a long, low wooden building that was functional rather than attractive, but because of the rough log siding, it fit nicely into the small rise upon which it rested. She noticed there was a long hitching rail outside the main door to the bunkhouse. Various sheds and lean-tos were obviously for storage; Amy saw the snout of a red tractor peeking out of one of them. There was the scent of horses and soil and fresh-cut hay in the air, and it was a natural and fitting aroma for the property of Jake Winter.

The late July sun had barely begun its downward arc, but the temperature was moderate for the time of year—about seventy-five—and the humidity was delightfully low. Though it was still early, the light seemed to have a dusk texture to it, softening hard edges and morphing brighter colors to hues closer to pastels.

Jake opened the front door before Amy had a chance to ring the doorbell. He looked good, she noticed, in jeans and a chambray shirt, and when he reached for the salad bowl, the fragrance of his aftershave tickled her nose. It was Clubman, she knew, because her father had used it for years. It was a spicy, masculine smell, radically different from the expensive colognes many of the men in the publishing world tended to wear.

"Quite a salad." Jake grinned. "There are only two of us, you know."

"Better too much than too little, right? I'm a major salad eater; I don't think much of this will go to waste." Amy followed Jake through the living room to the kitchen. She hadn't been in his home before, but there were no surprises for her there. She'd pictured this place in her mind in the course of the afternoon, and her musings had been close to perfect: masculine, leather couch and armchairs, a Remington reproduction on a wall, Indian throw rugs over shiny pine board floors, and a couple of tall bookcases, one on either side of the fireplace.

Jake put the salad in his refrigerator and poured two tall glasses of iced tea. "Let's sit in the living room for a bit," he suggested. Amy followed him out of the kitchen and walked to one of the bookshelves.

"You're a reader, I see—and no television set. Bravo."

"I have one," he admitted, "but it's in my bedroom. I haven't had it on since I don't know when. I relax with books—fiction almost exclusively. Light science fiction, Westerns, action-adventure, murder mysteries, all that stuff."

"I love mysteries too," Amy said.

They drifted into a comfortable, neighbor-to-neighbor conversation, touching on Amy's impressions of Cold-water, Jake's rodeo stock business, the weather, and whatever else came up.

When ice tinkled in their empty iced tea glasses, Jake suggested they get refills and go outside. "We can eat out there by the grill if you like," he said. "It's an awfully nice night."

"I'd like that," Amy said.

Sliding glass doors from the kitchen led to a small flagstone patio that held a picnic table, two lounge chairs, and a grill, which was smoking nicely, burning the charcoal to white embers.

"Tell me more about your business," Amy said.

His pride was obvious in his eyes and in his voice. "It's really pretty simple. Rodeo associations contact me and rent my horses and bulls for whatever number of days their events last. I have a horse that hasn't been ridden successfully in two years, and a bull that's never been ridden to the buzzer. I take good care of my animals, and rodeo folks know my stock will give the audience a show and the cowboys a good ride."

"A ride is eight seconds, right?"

"Yep. That seems short, but I'll tell you what: it seems like eight years when you're sitting on a rank bronc or bull that wants to get rid of you."

Amy smiled. "I guess you haven't tried to explain to a managing editor why you blew a deadline, then. I think I'd go with the horse or bull."

The conversation continued to drift casually from topic to topic. There was no indication of Jake's telephone nervousness in his demeanor; he was relaxed and obviously enjoying himself, just as Amy was.

The hamburgers were works of art. Each weighed close to a half pound, and the meat was ground sirloin rather than the more prosaic chuck. Oversized rolls—fresh from the bakery in Coldwater—lovingly held the big burgers. Jake offered thick slices of Bermuda onion and a spicy Chinese mustard as condiments. "No reason to put anything else on a burger," he said. "'Course, if you want ketchup, I'll get it for you." The way he said "ketchup" made it sound like a foul disease. "But"—he hesitated a dramatic beat—"I'll never feel right about having you over for burgers again."

"I wouldn't taint one of your masterpieces with ketchup," Amy promised. "This is probably the best hamburger I've ever eaten."

"Only 'probably'?"

They laughed together. Amy liked Jake's laugh; rich, full, a show of quick happiness. After dark they drank coffee in the living room. They both sat on the couch, not anywhere near touching, but each within the other's space. Both were at ease with that.

Amy glanced down at her watch and was amazed that it was 11:10. "I don't know where the time went," she said. "I know mornings around here get started early." She stood. "Thanks, Jake. This was fun. I hope we can do it again sometime—maybe at my place next."

Jake stood too and turned to face her. "Let's do that, Amy. I've had a great time. Hey—how about going riding day after tomorrow? I'm going to have the guys rolling your lawn, and the noise of their tractors would disturb your work anyway."

"Well . . . remember, I'm a beginner," she said as she walked out to her car. "But, I'd love to. Can we see the Indian mounds you mentioned?"

"Sure. I'll tell you what: come on over at about nine, and I'll have the horses saddled and ready to go."

At the door of her vehicle Jake reached out his hand to her, and she took it and held it for a moment. "Again, thanks. See you Friday," she said.

Jake nodded. "I'll see you then, Amy."

She sat on her couch at home after putting her Jeep in her garage. Nutsy, of course, found her lap immediately, even though she hadn't turned on any lights. It was good to review her evening in the dark, and the purring of her cat provided the perfect, peaceful background sound to her thoughts.

This move—all of this—was the right thing to do. My friends in New York were certain I was nuts—and maybe I was, at least according to their lifestyles. But this is right for me.

It was about 4:00 a.m. when Amy woke, her neck stiff from her position on the couch. She picked up Nutsy and found her way up the stairs and to her bedroom. Even as

51

she snuggled under the covers, the good feeling about the evening before was first in her mind.

She was up and sipping her first cup of coffee at 7:00 a.m. as she sat in front of her laptop. The early sun cascaded in her windows, and the slightest of breezes meandered in through the open windows. Morning sounds from Jake's ranch, muted and softened by the distance, reached her: the high-pitched whinny of a horse, the rumble of a tractor engine, the voice of one cowhand calling to another. Amy sat back from her work, thought for a long moment, and then stood and checked the pocket of her jeans for her Jeep keys. Riding was to be a brand-new experience for her. She didn't want Jake to think she was a complete klutz. She checked her kitchen clock: 8:35. She'd been sitting at her computer an hour and a half. She'd produced three sentences. She shook off the quick desperation that tried to take over her thoughts.

Coldwater Drug probably opens at nine, and the library probably does too. Amy fetched herself another cup of coffee and sipped at it until quarter to nine, then went to her garage.

She'd noticed the display of horse magazines just inside the door at the drugstore each time she'd stopped in, but she'd paid little attention to them other than a quick look at the horses on the covers. This morning she stopped in front of the rack and checked titles: *Western Horseman, Horse & Rider, Appaloosa News, Quarter Horse Journal,* and a slew of others interspersed with *Time, Newsweek, Redbook,* and other publications. Amy selected a half dozen equine-oriented magazines, paid at the counter, and headed for the library. There, using her new library card, she checked out an armload of books on western riding, amazed at the number of such references available on the shelves.

She'd always been a rapid, resourceful, and thorough researcher, and she approached Western riding with the same skills that had been so important to her in her TV work. She began with the parts of a Western saddle and used index cards to jot down bits of information. Then she moved on to the basics of riding: position in the saddle, hand use, cues to the horse, the various gaits, leg use in commands, trail-riding manners, and on and on. She stopped only once to wolf down a sandwich, and at 5:30 she had a headache, eye fatigue, and a full inch of index cards crammed with riding facts. It had been worth it: she still hadn't sat on the back of a horse with the reins in her hand, but she wouldn't sound like a disinterested novice when she talked with Jake in the morning.

That morning came quickly for Amy. By the time she'd showered, dressed, fed Nutsy, and eaten her customary bowl of corn flakes, her watch read a couple of minutes after seven. She sat at her laptop, but the words didn't seem to come to her—they were nudged aside by images of herself riding with Jake.

This is silly, she chided herself. *I guess I need to get out more—I feel like a sixteen-year-old waiting for her date to pick her up for the prom. Still—what a great way to spend a few hours, learning to ride out in the sunshine.*

Housework wasn't Amy's favorite thing, but it did serve to pass the time. She dusted, straightened, and vacuumed. She gathered up old newspapers and magazines and placed them in her recycling box. She investigated her refrigerator and threw out a piece of cheese that was green with mold and two slices of pizza she'd carefully wrapped in aluminum foil—over a month ago.

When Amy pulled in to the parking area behind Jake's home, she saw him standing in front of the steel building with a pair of saddled horses. She hurried to him.

"I hope I didn't keep you waiting, Jake." She smiled. "Good morning, by the way."

"Mornin'." Jake returned her smile. "You're right on time." He hesitated for a moment. "I hope this doesn't make a difference to you," he said, the slightest bit of worry in his voice, "but Wes says he needs to hold off on your lawn work at least another day—the low areas are still pretty wet."

"Not a problem at all. It'll get done when it gets done."

"Right." Jake smiled, looking relieved, Amy thought. He nodded toward the tall bay horse that was inspecting Amy with curiosity. "This ol' gal is Daisy—you'll ride her today. She's a quarter horse, thirteen years old, with the temperament of a kitten. Her gaits are smooth, and she doesn't have a silly or mean bone in her. She'll give you a good ride." He nodded toward the other horse. "This one's my Spike. He's also a quarter horse—a four-year-old. He's as wild as a hawk at times, but he's a good horse, and he's learning real fast. I'm going to be roping from him in a year or so."

Amy stepped forward and stroked Daisy's neck; the texture of the sleek, sun-warmed coat was something Amy hadn't experienced before. Daisy turned her head to look more closely at Amy. Impulsively, Amy kissed the mare's nose. "I like her," she said.

"'Course you do. C'mon, climb on and we'll get going."

Amy gathered the reins in her left hand and eased her left boot into the stirrup. She swung into the saddle in a single, smooth motion, surprising herself.

"I thought you didn't have any experience," Jake said. "You mount up like a cowhand."

"I did a little reading about Western riding," she admitted. "How far that'll take me once we're underway is up for grabs, I guess."

"You'll do fine," Jake said. He clucked to Spike, and the horse moved out at a walk. Without a command from Amy, Daisy followed the other horse, moving up to his side. The saddle creaked a bit under Amy, but Jake had adjusted the stirrups perfectly, and she sat comfortably, holding the reins a few inches over and ahead of the saddle horn as her references had told her to do.

Amy looked around her as they rode. The sky was the brilliant blue that even native Montanans marvel at, unmarred by any vestige of clouds. Around her, pastures spread lushly in all directions, washed of dust by the long rain. The day was perfect. When Jake asked if she wanted to jog a bit, Amy answered, "Sure," without hesitation.

She took a spanking for twenty yards or so. "Sit into the saddle, Amy," Jake urged. "You're moving against Daisy rather than with her. Let her carry you—don't fight her. Use your ankles kinda like the shock absorbers on a car. Let them take your weight instead of smacking the saddle with your bottom."

Amy nodded. Jake was right—the soles of her feet were pushing against the stirrups, making her legs rigid and transmitting the horse's movement to her upper body. She relaxed and began to find the rhythm of the jog. She glanced at Jake. He grinned. "Good," he said.

They tried the lope next. "This gait is just like riding a rocking chair," Jake explained. "Let your body move with Daisy just as you did in the jog. A good quarter horse can carry a rider at a lope all day long. They're famous for it. Remember, move with Daisy, not against her."

Amy quickly found the lope rhythm and was surprised to find that the motion was very much like that of being in a self-propelled rocking chair that Jake had mentioned. They alternated gaits for an hour or so with little conversation. Amy had no idea how far they'd gone and didn't really care. She was thoroughly enjoying herself and feeling good about her burgeoning riding skills.

Jake reined through a cluster of pines, and Daisy followed Spike. When they'd cleared the copse, Jake stopped and dismounted. "We'll tie the horses here and go on foot. The burial grounds aren't too far ahead."

They walked through another group of trees. The scent of pine was heavy in the air, and their boots crunched over many years of fallen needles and branches. It was cooler and darker in the woods, and the respite from the strength of the sun was welcome.

"I never ride up too close to the mounds," Jake said. "Seems kinda disrespectful somehow." He pointed. "There they are."

Two mounds, roughly the size of large automobiles, stood perhaps twenty feet apart. They were covered in grass, but the very tops appeared to be closer to raw dirt, brown against the green. Jake stopped, and Amy stopped next to him.

"What kind of Indians made these?" she asked.

"Crow, no doubt. Chiefs and shamans rated mounds like this, not braves or women. There were major ceremonies—dancing and everything—when the burials took place. After that, the grounds were considered sacred."

"Can we go a little closer?" Amy asked.

"Sure. As long as we don't disturb anything. These mounds and others like them are protected by the state of Montana. They're considered historical sites. The problem is that when the locations are revealed, the looters show up."

They took a few steps closer and stopped again. Amy experienced an odd sensation that she'd felt in the past when visiting the battleground at Gettysburg.

They kept the horses to a walk most of the way back, chatting or riding in silence, enjoying the day. When Jake's spread came into view as they topped a rise, he spoke again. "I'm trying something new in my business," he said. "I'm bringing in a cutting-horse trainer."

"Oh? I'm not sure what cutting horses are."

"Basically, they cut cattle—separate them from the herd—and direct them to where the cowboy needs them. There are big competitions for cutting horses, and a good one can earn his owner a ton of money. There's a good market for trained cutting horses. That's what I hope to tap into."

"When's this guy arriving?"

"A few days. And she's a woman. She comes with her own living quarters—a humongous trailer. Her name's Mallory—Mal—Powers. She's famous in training circles. I'm lucky to get her."

"I hope I get a chance to meet her," Amy said.

"You will—she'll be here probably six months or so. It'll be like having a new neighbor, at least for a while."

Amy couldn't help but notice the enthusiasm that crept into Jake's voice as he spoke of his new trainer. She nodded. "That'll be nice," she said.

At the barn Jake loosened the cinches of the two saddles.

"Can I walk Daisy to cool her down?" Amy asked.

"Nah," Jake said. "Neither one of them is hot. We walked almost all the way back. I'll rub them down a bit and turn them out to pasture." He looked at Amy. "I enjoyed this," he said. "You're a natural at riding. If you want to use Daisy again, just call here and one of the guys will bring her in and tack her up for you. As long as you keep my place in sight, you can ride wherever you like."

"Alone?"

Jake laughed. "Not alone. Daisy will be with you. Look—the way to learn to ride is to *ride*. So sure, anytime you want."

"Wow—that's great, Jake. Thanks. I'll certainly take you up on your offer. And I had a wonderful time today too."

The next morning the rush of sunshine into her room once again awakened Amy. She tossed back her covers, swung her legs to the side—and groaned. Both of her thighs felt as if someone had tied knots in the muscles, and her calves screamed at her when she attempted to stand next to her bed. Her legs were as stiff as two-by-fours, and her seat reminded her of the time she'd spent bouncing in the saddle before she'd caught on to the rhythm of the gaits. She hobbled to the bathroom, lurching as waves of pain grasped her legs in a vice-like grip. Nutsy cocked his head inquisitively at her.

"Riding pains," she grumbled to the cat, as if he'd asked her a question. "Not a big deal." She groaned again.

A very hot and overly long shower helped, at least to some degree. Amy stood to the rear of the stall, directed the showerhead on her legs, and let the heat and the gentle pounding do what they could. She dried and dressed, not bothering to even run a brush through her hair. She noticed as she limped down the stairs that she'd misbuttoned her blouse but decided not to worry about it. She made coffee, fed Nutsy, and sat glumly at the kitchen table. *A few hours of horseback riding and I'm a cripple? This is silly. I'm in good shape, I'm healthy—or am I? Is this going to happen every time I ride? If so, I'll stick to my Jeep.* She looked at the clock and then looked at it again. *Five after ten? I haven't slept this late in fifteen years. This is impossible. How can a few hours of riding—*

The chimes of the doorbell cut through her reverie. *I'm not home. No matter who it is, I'm not home. I'm in a rest home. I was taken away by ambulance because I couldn't walk. I have a rare leg disease.*

The chimes sounded again. Amy stood and hobbled to the door. Through the peephole she saw a handsome, casually dressed man about her age looking back at her. Maggie Lane stood next to him. They were both smiling.

"Hi, Amy," the guy said, apparently seeing her eye at the peephole. "I'm Ian Lane—Reverend Ian Lane. You've met my wife, Maggie. We stopped by to say hello, to welcome you to Coldwater. Got a minute to chat?"

Amy panicked. Excuses that might chase them away raced through her mind, and none of them worked. She pawed at her almost-dry, flyaway hair and looked down at the strange way her blouse was gathered—kind of bunched—at her stomach.

"Amy?"

She opened the door and forced a smile. "Hi, Reverend Lane. Hi, Maggie. Come on in. You're in luck; I just made some coffee."

Ian's smile slipped away for a millisecond, and his eyes showed his confusion as he looked at her. "Umm, sure," he said. "Coffee sounds good. If it's no trouble, I mean."

"No trouble. Come on." Amy turned away, leading the couple to the kitchen, acutely aware of how ludicrous her short, baby steps must look to them.

"Amy?" Maggie asked, her voice conveying concern. "Are you OK? Is this a bad time? We should've called first, but we were driving right by and . . ."

"We'd be happy to stop another time," Ian said.

Amy collapsed into the chair she'd vacated. She sighed. "Reverend . . ."

"Please—Ian."

"Ian, then. I went horseback riding for several hours yesterday. I'd never been on a horse before. Today I feel like I've played a full game in the National Football League. I need a pair of leg transplants."

Maggie took the Mr. Coffee carafe and topped off Amy's cup. She opened a cupboard, removed two cups, and poured for herself and Ian. "I hope I'm not being too presumptuous, but you don't look like you're ready to play hostess."

"I'm not—and thanks, Maggie."

Ian had settled into a chair across the table from Amy. Maggie sat to her right, looking concerned. "Let me tell you a story," Ian said. "I know you met Maggie. You may or may not know that she runs a horse operation, is a barrel racer, and was almost born on horseback. We went riding together one day when I was courting her, and it was my first time." He smiled. "I know exactly what's going on with you. I thought I was going to die. I learned that riding uses a bunch of muscles that simply don't get used like that otherwise. For what it's worth, it'll go away in a day or so. I promise."

"But does it happen every time? I don't think I can go through this again."

Maggie and Ian laughed, but there was only kindness in the sound.

"No, no, no!" Maggie promised. "The more you ride, the less you'll stiffen up."

For the first time that day, Amy's face showed a real smile—one she actually felt. "Whew. That's a relief." She paused for a moment and looked at her guests. "I guess I'm not much of a country girl."

"You can't learn everything there is to learn about the West immediately. It takes some time," Maggie said.

"Well, I've got lots of time, anyway. And I'm a quick learner."

"Good," Ian said. "Say, who were you riding with?"

"Jake Winter from the next place over. He let me use a nice old mare named Daisy. She's a sweetheart. We took quite a ride."

"You couldn't have had a better riding instructor," Ian said. "When it comes to horses, even Maggie looks up to Jake."

Maggie nodded, agreeing. "And Jake takes wonderful care of his animals."

"I saw that yesterday," Amy said. "The way he was with his horse and with Daisy."

"Look," Maggie said, "we need to get out of your hair, Amy. We'll get our house tour next time. You need to soak in a hot tub and take it easy."

"I'm sorry I wasn't better prepared for you guys," Amy said. "Please come back soon."

"We will, Amy," Ian said. "And our church is open to you, of course. Sunday services are at nine and eleven."

Maggie stood from her chair and Ian did too.

"Stay where you are. We'll let ourselves out," Maggie said.

Amy took the advice about the soak. After Maggie and Ian left, she lurched her way up the stairs and into her bathroom. She peered into the mirror. Her hair looked as if there'd been an explosion on her head. The bunched blouse made her cringe.

She groaned and bent to start the hot water running into the tub.

3

On yet another spectacular Montana morning two days later, Amy took her breakfast coffee outside. She was walking much easier than she had for the past forty-eight hours. Her muscles had stopped arguing with her, the pain in her legs was gone, and amazingly enough, she was actually looking forward to riding again.

She stopped short as she stepped out onto her porch; she'd gotten a new neighbor overnight. Curious, Amy walked to the fence separating Jake's property from her own. Beyond the pasture, tucked next to the steel building, was a large—almost mobile-home-sized—travel trailer. Amy had no skill in estimating the length of such rigs, but she didn't need skill to tell that this unit was not only large but also expensive. It seemed to avoid the boxiness of standard travel trailers and was instead smoothly streamlined in appearance. The side facing Amy had a long awning that obviously swung out from a compartment below the roof, and there was a grill and several lawn chairs under the awning. A cable TV antenna protruded from the roof, looking like a miniature radar tower. She noticed that the windows facing her had no air-conditioning units, which surprised her until she saw the rectangular AC housing on the roof. *All the comforts of home*, she mused.

The clip-clop of a shod horse drew Amy's attention to the road. Wes Newton, riding a tall gray horse, waved to her and turned his mount into her driveway, jigging his gait from the walk to a jog. Amy sipped her coffee as the cowhand rode toward her, his eyes sweeping over her lawn.

Wes drew rein a few feet from Amy and offered her a smile. "Mornin', Miss Amy," he drawled.

"Morning yourself, Wes." Amy smiled. "How about a cup of coffee? I have a fresh pot in the kitchen."

"It's a rare day I turn down an offer like that, Miss Amy—black, please." He nodded toward the lawn. "While you fetch the java I'm going to look over the grass a bit. I figured on bringing the rollers over today and getting this mess fixed up for you. Jake, he figured we could do it a bit sooner, but I argued him out of it. I tol' him the ground wasn't ready yet. He's all in a lather to get the job done."

As Amy turned toward her front door to pour the coffee, Wes added, "He got a half dozen of them bushes too."

She turned back. "Six? Only four of mine were damaged, and one of those wasn't completely wrecked. I don't need—"

"Yes'm," Wes interrupted. "That's what I tol' Jake. Sometimes talking to him is like talking to a fence post. Anyways, you're getting six new bushes."

"I'll see if I can change his mind," Amy said.

Wes nodded as he swung down from his saddle. "Sure," he grunted. He dropped the reins in front of his horse, said, "Stand," and walked away from the animal. The horse didn't move, and when Amy came back out with Wes's coffee and a fresh cup for herself, the gray was in precisely the same place he'd been left. Wes completed his walk around the lawn and accepted the mug from Amy. She noticed he held it in both hands as he took a long drink. Amy cringed. The coffee was still steaming hot. She'd seen the cowhands in Drago's drinking their coffee the same way, gulping it down fresh from the pot, as if it were a cold soft drink. Most of them, too, held the mug in both their hands.

"Ground's good, Miss Amy. We'll be back in a half hour or so."

"Fine, Wes. Thanks." She looked over at the travel trailer. "That's Jake's new trainer, right? Mallory Powers?"

"Yes'm. Quite a rig, ain't it?"

"It sure is. I've never seen one like it before."

"You won't see another one, neither. Mal had this one custom built. She's particular about stuff."

"You know her, Wes?"

He took another drink from his mug. "I know her," he said. A long moment later he added, "I knew her pa too. She's a good trainer—has a gentle hand with horses." Amy waited for the "But . . ." that all but hung in the air between them like a neon sign. When Wes didn't comment further she was mildly disappointed and more than mildly curious about Mallory Powers.

❧❧

Working on her novel was impossible with the snarling and growling of the machinery outside. Amy pushed out from the kitchen table, switched off her laptop, and went to watch the process of returning her lawn to its pre-horse-invasion state.

There were two cowboys on four-wheeled ATVs towing fifty-five-gallon barrel-sized rollers behind their machines. The men worked well together, one running horizontal lines across the lawn, the other vertical. The gaping indentations were disappearing rapidly, leaving nothing in their places except slightly scuffed dirt and some dead grass. A cowhand on foot with a large sack was casting seed onto the bare spots. A small backhoe with a wagon behind it was using its scoop to pluck out the damaged bushes. The wagon contained six new bushes, their roots wrapped in wet burlap. The fellow on the backhoe let his machine idle as he studied the sheet of paper he held. Amy rushed up to him.

"I don't really need six new bushes," she said. "I'm sure Jake can take two of these back and get credit for them."

The driver—Amy could see now he was quite young—shook his head, grinned, and held the paper out to Amy. She took it from him. It was a rough drawing of the length of her driveway with dark *X*s to indicate which bushes should be replaced. Underneath the diagram, in neat handwriting were the words: *Don't let Ms. Hawkins scare you away. I want all six of these bushes planted.* It was signed simply, "Jake."

"Well," Amy said. "I guess you've got your orders."

68

"Sure do," the young fellow agreed. "Now, if you'll excuse me, I'll get back to work."

Within a pair of hours Amy's home was quiet once again. Her lawn looked better than it had since it'd been planted, and the driveway snaked its way through the neat lines of green shrubs. She stood on her porch for several minutes taking in and thoroughly enjoying the work done. Then, she nodded to herself, walked to her garage, fired up her Jeep, and headed for Coldwater.

Ingram's Book Nook was at the end of Main Street in town, housed in a rather small building that had once, many years ago, been a saddle and tack repair shop. Now it was lined with wooden bookshelves and two sale item tables and scattered overstuffed chairs with floor lamps positioned next to them. There was a store cat named Kafka who alternated his time between sleeping on the display in the front window, patrolling the store for mice, and batting a cherished golf ball around the shop. Amy loved the place and had since the first time she'd walked in the door.

The shelf of horse books was long and well stocked. After much consideration, Amy selected a novel titled *A Good Horse and a Three Dollar Compass*, which was the story of a long and arduous ride made by a young Texas physician in the 1870s through a blizzard, in order to save the life of a young mother. Amy paid at the counter, scratched between Kafka's ears, and went out to her vehicle.

Jake's truck was in the driveway, and Wes was sitting outside the steel building, just as he had been the day Jake's horses had torn up her lawn. "Jake around?" she asked after greeting Wes with a smile.

"Right where you found him last time," Wes said. "He's watching Mal work with a horse. Go on back."

The building was less intimidating this time. Amy walked through the business area, the book tucked under her arm, and along the aisle leading to the central arena. As she approached the door she felt the thudding of hooves in the soles of her loafers. She tugged open the door, entered the arena, and walked up to stand next to Jake. He didn't notice her, so tight was his focus on the horse in the dirt-floored enclosure. She stood back a half step and a foot to his side. Her eyes ran over the side of Jake's face, the length of his lean body, the forward tilt of the brim of his Stetson before she looked away, afraid he'd catch her inspecting him. He didn't; he was still unaware of her standing there, and his gaze was still riveted to the horse.

Or is it the rider he's so intent on? Hard to tell. If I were a man, I'd sure be watching her.

Mallory Powers's straight, honey-blonde hair was a bit more than shoulder length, and it flowed behind her as she rode. Even at a distance, Amy could see that the woman's face was a classic of contemporary beauty: fine cheekbones, a nose that was small and perfectly straight, large eyes, no doubt blue, with long, luxurious lashes, rather thin lips that were now tight in concentration. It was easy to see that Mallory was tall—perhaps five-foot-ten, like Amy—even as she sat in the saddle. Her long, jean-clad legs promised to be as tightly muscled as were her arms, which were visible in the sleeveless blouse she wore. Amy noticed the woman's boots. They were Western rather than cowboy, with a lightly stitched design against the tan of the leather but no other decoration. They were practical and serviceable but quite feminine too. They made a positive statement about the woman who wore them. Amy looked down at her own fashionable loafers and grimaced to herself.

The thought struck Amy that Mallory would be at home in an L. L. Bean advertisement, wearing a fancy backpack and paired with a ruggedly handsome, forest-ranger type.

Amy poked Jake's arm lightly with the edge of the novel, and he turned to her, startled. His face broke immediately into a grin. "Amy, good to see you." He looked at the book. "What's this?"

"It's for you. A little thank-you gift for having my place put back together."

"You didn't have to do that," he said.

"You didn't have to replace all six of my bushes, either. Here, take it."

Jake took the book gently from her hand and inspected the cover. "I read about this story in *Western Horseman*. I've been meaning to stop in town and pick it up or order it. Thanks, Amy, thanks a lot. I know I'll enjoy it."

His obvious enthusiasm over the novel brought a broad smile to Amy's face. "I hope so. That's why I got it for you."

"See? A pretty lady shows up, and Jake forgets all about me," said a mock-pouty voice. "I'm really hurt."

Amy and Jake both shifted their attention from one an-

71

other to Mallory Powers, who was sitting on the horse a few feet from them.

"Not hardly." Jake laughed. "You've got that horse changing leads like a champion," he said. "Mallory, meet my friend and next-door neighbor, Amy Hawkins."

Amy had been right—Mallory's eyes were blue, but a blue rarely seen. It was deep, almost indigo, and there were tiny sparkles of gold. The effect was stunning.

"Pleased to meet you, Mallory," Amy said. "Jake told me about you."

"Nothing bad, I hope." Mallory smiled. Her teeth, of course, were almost startlingly white and perfectly even.

"Not a thing; he told me how much he was looking forward to having you here."

"Hey, look," Jake said. "I promised to make Mal one of my world-famous burgers tonight. Can you come over and join us, Amy?"

Amy's eyes flicked to those of Mallory, and she wasn't quite sure if she'd actually seen the very rapid infusion of heat that was gone as quickly as it appeared.

"The more the merrier," Mal said.

"I'd love to," Amy said. "How about if I bring the salad again?"

"Sure, that'll be great. About 6:30?" Jake said.

"OK then," Amy said. "I need to scoot. I have an errand to run in town. Mallory, nice meeting you. See you both this evening."

"Nice meeting you, Amy," Mallory said. For whatever reason, her smile didn't seem to reach her eyes.

Amy's Jeep was filled with the smell of new leather, but she enjoyed the aroma and didn't turn on the air or open her window any farther. Knipper's Boots 'n' Shoes had quite a selection of boots, and Amy found a pair she immediately fell in love with. They were similar in cut and conservative design to those Mallory Powers wore, but the leather was a deeper, almost chocolate color. Amy reached over and patted the box printed with the name "Justin" and smiled to herself. "Justins are the top of the line in boots," Mr. Knipper had told her. "They'll last darn near forever and still look good."

Amy sincerely hoped so.

Amy set out in her Jeep with her bowl of salad next to her on the passenger seat at 6:25. As she swung into Jake's driveway, she wondered why she'd driven the relatively short distance. It was a delightful evening; a sweet little breeze that smelled of grass and fertile soil was chasing off the heat of the afternoon.

City ways, I guess. Just like wearing yuppie loafers instead of boots. She sighed but then brightened as she parked behind Jake's pickup. *But I'm learning.*

The aroma of the briquettes and of the small, brittle branches of mesquite Jake always included in his grill fires reached around the corner of the house and beckoned Amy.

Jake was in a lounge chair, a tall glass of iced tea in his hand. He stood as Amy walked to the picnic table and put down her salad. "Perfect night for a cookout, isn't it?" he said.

"Only thing that makes it better is having you here to share it." Amy noticed the quick flush that came to Jake's face with the compliment, and it somehow made his words even more appreciated.

"That's sweet of you to say, Jake. I'm happy to be here and very pleased you invited me."

There was a short but not uncomfortable silence as their eyes met and held. Then, Jake said, "Have a seat. I'll take your salad in and put it in the refrigerator." He nodded toward the table. "I cut up some vegetables, and that dip's real good. I'll bring you a glass of iced tea—or would you rather have a Diet Pepsi or something? Coffee?"

"Tea would be great," Amy said, sitting at the table. "I'll try some of the veggies and dip." She selected a three-inch piece of celery, used its length as a scoop into the reddish, salsa-looking dip, and took a bite. Her eyes teared almost instantaneously, and she felt as if she'd stuffed an ember from Jake's grill into her mouth. Her throat constricted. The house and kitchen were nearby—but what would her host think? She looked around frantically, sweat streaming down her forehead as if she were standing hatless in the Sahara on the hottest day of the year.

There was a length of green garden hose under a spigot on the side of the house, she remembered. She ran to it, looked around quickly, spit the celery and dip onto the ground, and turned on the water. It was warm and murky and tasted like rubber—and it was wonderful. She turned the spigot handle a bit more to increase the flow of water and rinsed the inside of her mouth.

"You must be awful thirsty, Amy." The word *awful* was stretched out in exaggeration.

Amy choked, dropped the hose from her mouth, and looked up to see Mallory standing a yard away from her.

"The dip," Amy choked out. "It surprised me."

Mallory waited a beat. "Are you OK now?"

Amy turned off the hose and wiped her hand across her mouth. "Sure. I'll be right along—you go ahead."

Mallory smiled again and walked around the corner of the house. Amy straightened her blouse, wiped her face again, and returned to the picnic table. Jake was in a lawn chair, and Mallory had pulled another chair around so that it faced him.

"I'm sorry, Amy," Jake said. "I should have warned you about the dip. It's pretty potent stuff. Do you want some ice water?"

"No, my tea will do fine. And I should have remembered that chili peppers and cayenne are favored out here." She smiled. "I'll try it again later, but in a very small dose."

Jake's eyes met hers. "Well, I'm really sorry. I just didn't think."

Amy took a long drink of the iced tea. It felt wonderful in her mouth and on her throat. "Forget it." She smiled. "I'm still getting used to Montana."

"Takes a while," he said.

Mallory's face was a study in innocence. "Takes some people longer than others," she said. After a moment, she said, "I'm sure you'll catch on to things . . . eventually."

Mallory was being perfectly polite, but Amy couldn't help but feel as if Mallory viewed her as an enemy.

75

Despite Amy's sudden unease around the other woman, the meal went well. Jake's burgers were perfectly cooked, the bakery rolls were fresh, and Amy's salad was a success, as simple as it was. The conversation ebbed and flowed smoothly. They discussed the weather, current events, books, and the unhappy state of national politics. And whatever Amy seemed to have seen in Mallory's speech earlier had disappeared. The woman appeared genuinely interested in Amy's writing background and the fact that she was now laboring on her first novel. *Maybe she was just uncomfortable*, Amy thought. *Or maybe I was too quick to judge, since I felt like such a dolt.*

"Tell me about your career," Amy suggested. "Jake says you're a very well-known and respected trainer."

Mallory's smile was self-deprecating, almost shy. "I've had good horses to work with," she said. "When I started out with my father's stock, I didn't know what I was doing. But I got lucky along the way and learned training from some of the superstars—friends of my dad's."

"Your family is in horses, then?"

"Oh yeah. Powers Ranch & Show Horses was started back in the 1940s, and it's been growing ever since. I probably rode before I could walk. In fact, I know I did—there's an old photo of me sitting in a saddle on a pony's back, and I don't look all of a year old in it."

"Speaking of riding," Jake said, "you haven't taken me up on my offer to use Daisy again, Amy. That wasn't just a polite offer, you know. The ol' gal could use the exercise, and you can learn a lot picking around on the trails."

"I haven't forgotten your offer—and I'll take you up on it

soon. I've been putting some long hours in on my novel, and that doesn't leave me much time." *Or long hours sitting at my kitchen table doing nothing but staring at my keyboard.*

Mal leaned forward in her chair and put her hand on Jake's forearm. "I can't imagine writing a book, can you, Jake?"

Jake considered for a long moment. "Nope. I can't say that I can."

"And I can't imagine riding like you, Jake, or training horses like you, Mallory. I guess each of us has our skills," Amy said. "Also, there's a whole lot of difference between writing a novel and writing a novel that gets the attention of reviewers and readers." She met Mallory's gaze. "That's the hard part. Sometimes, too, the book seems to be . . ." She stopped, self-conscious, not wanting to reveal what was happening with *The Longest Years.*

"Be what, Amy?" Jake asked.

"Sometimes it kind of stalls for a little bit," she said, forcing a smile.

The sun had eased down below the horizon as they talked. The picnic table was littered with empty iced tea glasses and three coffee cups that'd been refilled twice in the course of the evening. Jake yawned behind his hand and looked at the women guiltily to see if either had noticed. Both had.

Mallory checked her wristwatch. "Looks like it's time to call it a night," she said. "But Jake, you haven't seen the inside of my new trailer yet. Want to take a quick peek?"

"I'd really like to see it too," Amy said.

Mallory's eyes flashed hotly for the briefest part of a second and then became calm once again. "Sure. Let's head over there now."

They walked through the burgeoning darkness with Jake walking between Amy and Mallory. The trailer seemed graceless and lumpish in the dwindling light, at least to Amy.

Mal took a set of keys from the pocket of her jeans and pressed a button. A light over the front door clicked on, as did lights at either end of the trailer and along its front, splashing illumination around the unit.

"Neat," Jake observed. "Like the ignitions on the new cars and trucks."

Amy and Jake stood back as Mal fit a key to the lock of the front door and swung it open. She waved her arm theatrically. "Come on in, folks—I'll give you the grand tour of my castle."

The interior was strangely expansive, given the dimensions of the trailer. The couch and two chairs were leather; the carpet a rich Berber. Bookshelves were placed against two walls. A flat-screen TV was set into the wall between the living room and kitchen. Below the screen were shelves holding a high-end sound system.

Mallory led them into the kitchen. It was a bit crowded, but it accommodated all three of them. The range was brushed metal, as was the sink. The refrigerator was a stark, flat black. A microwave was suspended beneath a counter. The countertops were marble.

"This seems really comfortable, Mallory," Amy said honestly. "I guess I expected ... well, I'm not sure what I expected."

Jake was fascinated by the allocation of space and the feeling of openness that was radically different from any trailer he'd ever been in, mobile or stationary. "Did you design the interior, Mal?" he asked.

Mallory laughed, moved a step closer to Jake, and put both hands on his arm for a moment. "Thanks for the compliment, Jake. I wish I had," she chortled. "But no, I hired an architect who specializes in these types of things."

The bedroom easily contained a queen-sized bed and a dresser. The bath wasn't spacious, but it offered both tub and shower. The sink was marble. The remaining small area—not much larger than a sizable and deep closet—which Mallory described as the den, held a small desk, a computer and monitor, and two upright, three-drawer filing cabinets. The framed pictures on the wall were of cutting horses at work in arenas before stands full of people. Mallory was the rider in most of them.

The tour ended back in the living room. Amy crouched and checked titles of the books on the shelves while Mal and Jake discussed the work planned for the next day. The conversation buzzed to the side as Amy pulled the occasional novel off a shelf. What looked like a leather-bound collection of the full works of William Shakespeare turned out to be a prop—a device made to look like a series of books on a shelf. She had to swallow the grin that had spread across her face before she turned back to Jake and Mallory.

"Good," Jake said, a note of finality in his voice. "We're agreed that Lancer's Trifle is a good prospect and you'll spend some time with him."

"He's a good horse, Jake. His sire is as dumb as a fence

post, but Lancer seems willing. I guess we'll see how bright he is as we go on. If he doesn't work out, you've got other good stock."

"Amy?" Jake called. "You about ready to go?"

She stood from the bookshelf and walked to the door, where Mal and Jake stood. "Thanks for showing me your place, Mal," she said. "I'm really impressed."

"Me too," Jake agreed. "See you in the morning, right?"

"Right. 'Night, Amy."

When the door was closed, Jake and Amy walked back toward Jake's home. The night was as quiet as most Montana nights were, and Amy was getting used to the silence. They walked about half the way without speaking.

"Nice trailer," Jake said, sounding as if he'd been searching for some way to break the silence.

"Nice," Amy agreed.

"So, what do you think of Mallory?" Jake asked.

"She's an interesting person. And she seems very competent at what she does. Do you know her well?" she asked.

They continued walking as they talked, their boots moving silently in the grass.

"Not really, no. I met her a couple of times at rodeos." He stopped there, making it clear he didn't have a whole lot more to say on the subject.

"Really? She seems to know you well." Suddenly she regretted saying it. "I'm sorry, it's none of my business," she said as she felt her face flush red.

Jake stopped, and Amy did too. In a moment he took a half step and turned to face Amy. "I met her father about eight or so years ago. Her mother, I later learned, died shortly after Mal was born. Stuart Powers—her father—was one of the most unlikable men I've ever met—avaricious, unyielding, not particularly good to his horses. Don't get me wrong—he wasn't cruel to them, didn't neglect them. But for someone in the business of raising and training horses, he never seemed to really care about them. He was hard on his daughter, I've heard. *Distant* is one word folks use to describe how he treated her. Like she was a hired hand who was barely worth keeping on the payroll." He paused before continuing. "He died six months ago."

"She's done well even in spite of her father though, hasn't she?"

"Yeah. Regardless of Stuart, she became a top trainer. It hasn't been easy for her."

They walked to Amy's Jeep, neither speaking until Amy turned at her vehicle door. "This was fun, Jake. I enjoyed myself."

Jake extended his hand for the friendly shake they'd parted with in the past. "I . . . well . . . this was fun, Amy. Thanks for coming over, and for welcoming Mallory."

"I had a good time," Amy said. "Thanks for having me." She smiled at him. "See you soon."

"You bet," Jake said.

"Well," Amy said aloud as she drove down Jake's driveway to the road. "Well," she repeated as she turned into her own driveway a few moments later and tucked her vehicle into its spot in the garage. Instead of entering through the garage to the kitchen door, Amy walked out through the overhead, leaving it up, and sat on her porch step. Across her side yard and beyond Jake's fence and pasture, she could see the glow of a light in Jake's living room. There were no lights showing in Mallory's trailer.

A cool, almost chilly, breeze sent Amy across the porch and in her front door. She clicked on the lamp at the end of the couch. Nutsy attacked one of her new boots from under the love seat, shooting out hissing in mock ferocity, wrapping his front paws around her ankle, digging at the leather with his hind paws.

"Swell," she said to the kitten. "I forgot to leave a light on for you, so you slept all night. And now it's playtime, right? Whether I want to sleep or not?"

Nutsy released the boot and hustled back under the love seat, his eyes glinting like black marbles as he glared at his quarry. Amy started for the kitchen. She'd taken only a couple of steps before being attacked again. She sighed through a smile. It had been an interesting and in some ways perplexing night.

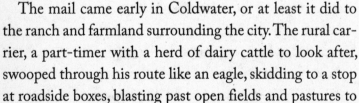

The mail came early in Coldwater, or at least it did to the ranch and farmland surrounding the city. The rural carrier, a part-timer with a herd of dairy cattle to look after, swooped through his route like an eagle, skidding to a stop at roadside boxes, blasting past open fields and pastures to the next box, and the next, often leaving the post office in full dark to begin his rounds.

Amy had gotten into the habit of taking her first cup of coffee outside on the pleasant summer days that seemed to be following one another without a break. It was a part of the day she cherished, perhaps because it was so conspicuously free of the rush and hustle that had started her days not too long ago.

She stood in her backyard and watched a few of Jake's mares arguing about something, their high-pitched squealing sharp and angry. She'd long since gotten used to the pasture squabbles and had grown to enjoy watching the horses and their own closed little society with its tightly established pecking order.

The rumble of a blown exhaust system brought Amy to her feet from her porch and started her toward the mailbox at the roadside in front of her home. The deceleration of the carrier's engine indicated that he had something for her. The carrier slid to a stop at her box and then, almost instantly, was blasting on down the road again with a cloud of dust and grit in his wake.

Amy checked the sole piece of mail she took from her box: "Lloyd Hampton Sturgiss, Literary Agent, 417 Madison Avenue, New York, New York, 10016" stood out crisply as the return address. She opened the letter right there at the mailbox. The text was in a script font on thick, creamy paper.

Dear Amy,

Just a brief note to see how things are going with you and how Longest is progressing. As I mentioned to you at lunch the last time we met, we were very fortunate to contract with Meadowdale

Publishing Group. They've never been prone to taking on newer writers who can't show extensive track histories. Nevertheless, your editors there have great faith in you and in how Longest will impact the market.

Of course, the schedule you and I structured several months ago isn't carved in stone. I realize that delays can take place. Still, the completed first half of the novel was due last week. I hope you'll get those pages to me quickly so that I can meet again with Meadowdale to further discuss promotion, signings, and the postpub tour.

I'll watch for the manuscript, Amy. If there are any problems, give me a call here or in my California office, where I'll be for the next two or three weeks.

Very best regards,

The agent's signature was an indecipherable scrawl under the closing. Amy looked at it longer than she needed to. Then, she turned back to her house. It seemed like a long walk.

4

Amy was going stir-crazy. Her home had somehow become smaller, and her pacing somehow reduced it in size even more. Her laptop seemed to goad her from its spot on the kitchen table when she wasn't sitting at it with her fingers poised over the keyboard. The problem was, she was spending long and arduous hours on her novel with little production to show for her time. She was confused. Her editing work had never come to such an impasse, been so acutely frustrating. And Lloyd Sturgiss's words seemed to hang over the back of her neck like a blade. His politely phrased, nonconfrontational letter said more between the lines than it did in its actual text, the message being: get in gear or you'll blow this contract, lady.

The sharp ringing of steel-shod hooves in her driveway drew Amy to her front window. Wes was just swinging down from his horse, a rangy chestnut with a pure white stripe along its muzzle. Amy hurried through the process of grinding a handful of beans, started the Mr. Coffee, and went out the front door. Wes had ground-tied his mount and walked out onto Amy's lawn. He saw Amy and called, "It's lookin' good, Miss Amy."

"It sure is," Amy agreed as she watched Wes walk back to the driveway. He had the stride of many of the men she saw in Coldwater—bowlegged, slow, and kind of rolling, as if he was uncomfortable being off his horse. "Coffee, Wes?" she called to him.

"You betcha," he said with a grin. "'Specially when you make such a nice, strong cup. Some of this coffee 'round here—it's got no more kick to it than a cup of dishwater."

"No danger of that with my brew," Amy responded as she headed for the house. Within a couple of minutes she returned to the driveway, a steaming mug in each hand. Wes accepted his, thanked her, and took a long, satisfying series of gulps. Amy cringed. The coffee was barely a minute from the pot.

Wes noticed the look on Amy's face. "You're wonderin' why I go after my coffee like that," he said. "It's an old habit. A man learns to drink coffee like that when he works with cattle or horses. There's always somethin' that needs to be done right this very second on a spread, and if a guy can't slug down his java, he's probably not going to get much of it."

"I learn something new about the West every day," Amy said. *And about sweet old cowboys with very good manners too.*

Wes's eyes seemed to sparkle a bit as he said, "Seems like you learned Jake makes the best hamburgers in Montana. An' it looks like he kinda likes havin' you around, Miss Amy."

"I enjoy Jake's company. He's an interesting guy."

There seemed to be more on Wes's mind. Amy decided to wait him out, so she just sipped at her coffee.

He cleared his throat. "He is that," he said. "You been with him, what . . . three times, now? An' one of those times was goin' ridin'. See, Jake isn't much on going out. Dating and so forth. I suspect he likes you well enough. That'd be my guess."

Amy had no idea where this was going, but Wes's discomfort was becoming more obvious to her. She didn't speak, not knowing how to respond and not understanding the cowboy's point.

The old fellow blushed—the color was apparent even under his decades-old tan. "I like you, Miss Amy. Otherwise, I wouldn't have said what I jus' did about Jake."

"Well, anything you say to me stays with me."

"There's somethin' else I gotta say. This ain't my business, but I need to say it. You watch out for Mallory Powers. She's had her eye on Jake for a few years now, and she ain't one to take no for an answer, no matter what Jake wants."

Amy thought maybe Wes was exaggerating. "But Jake invited her here to work for him, didn't he? She didn't just roll in and set up her trailer on her own. So . . ."

Wes waved a hand, chasing the subject away in the same manner he'd chase a pesky horsefly. "We'll talk on her another time," he mumbled as he fit a boot into a stirrup.

Amy nodded. *Well, OK.*

From his seat in his saddle, Wes said, "I see you got that little lawn chair out in back of your garage. You'd best bring it inside before tomorrow, or it'll get blown all the way to Missoula."

Amy scanned the sky. It was a peaceful delft blue from horizon to horizon, without any sort of cloud cover. The sun beat down with its summer strength, and the air was dead calm. "A storm coming? What makes you think that?"

"Yup, there's a storm comin', and she'll be more'n what we saw a couple weeks ago. That was just rain. This one will have some teeth in it." He pointed toward the pasture, where several horses grazed placidly. "See how them mares are kinda sticking closer than they usually do to one another? That's the herd instinct showing itself—gathering up when they're threatened. It means something's comin'. Plus, my knee is aching pretty good, and that's a sure sign of weather on its way." He looked up at the sky for a long moment. "One other way too," he said.

"Oh?"

"Yeah. The Montana Weather Service has an advisory out for our parts. Those boys aren't often wrong."

Amy laughed. "I'd hoped this good weather would never end."

"It'll be back," Wes promised. He tipped his Stetson, turned his horse, and headed down the driveway to the road. Amy watched him, smiling. *What a sweetheart he is.*

She started toward her porch and then stopped and detoured to her backyard. There, she folded her lawn chair and tucked it away inside the garage. She'd barely entered her home through the garage when the front doorbell rang. A

UPS driver smiled at her when she opened the door. She signed his invoice and accepted the package.

It contained four books. She took them from the cardboard box and placed them on her couch. Amy didn't recognize the titles or the authors of any of them, but the logo of Meadowdale Publishing Group was prominent on the accompanying short letter. Like all other publishers, Meadowdale liked to keep its writers apprised of what was being published by them in the writers' genre or specialty area. She looked at the titles and skimmed the blurbs on the back cover of each book. They were historic novels, set in various periods of time, each with a female protagonist, much like Amy's *The Longest Years*.

All writers read voraciously, she knew. At a mystery conference she'd once heard Sara Paretsky say about her own reading habits, "In a sense, it's almost like low-key plagiarism. I pick up a little twist of language, a tiny bit of description, and then build on them in my own mind until they come out in new forms in my writing. And if that doesn't happen, but I enjoy the book, I'm way ahead of the game—I've escaped into a good story."

Amy chose one of the four novels at random, settled into the love seat adjacent to the fireplace, and immersed herself in its pages. It was a strong and compelling story with believable characters and lots of action, and she was unaware of the time passing until she found herself rubbing at her eyes and squinting at the pages of the book. Much of the afternoon had passed as she read, and it was now dusk.

She set the novel aside, stood, and stretched to chase the stiffness from her back.

Nutsy, awakened from a nap by Amy's moving around, rubbed against her ankles, purring. When she took a step toward the kitchen, the cat charged ahead of her, anticipating the possibility of a treat. He guessed right. Amy tossed a couple of Whisker Lickin's nuggets—Nutsy's all-time favorite snack—on the floor near his dishes. For herself she made a thick tuna fish sandwich and poured a glass of iced tea. She sat at the kitchen table at her laptop and clicked it on. She reviewed some of the scenes and dialogue she'd written at her last session as she ate her sandwich and sipped at her tea.

Some of the material was at least passable, but much of it simply wasn't. After a few minutes she clicked off the computer and carried her plate and glass to the sink, rinsed them, and put them on her drainer. She looked out the window over the sink without really seeing much of anything, deep in thought about her novel. Then, the strange quality of the light, and the dark, subdued hues at the western horizon caught her attention. The sunsets were always beautiful and frequently spectacular in Montana, Amy had discovered. She'd never seen one quite like tonight's, though. It was as if the vibrant colors had been drained from the sky and replaced with somber shades of gray. The light, too, was different. It was a clear night, yet somehow the light had an indistinct quality to it, as if she was seeing everything through light gauze. Amy left the kitchen and turned on the overhead light as she entered the living room. She situated herself in the love seat once again and opened the book to the scrap of paper she'd used as a bookmark.

The unmistakable ratcheting sound of Nutsy vomiting pulled Amy from the book. *Just another hairball? Or did he get into something he shouldn't have and he's really sick?* She found him huddled in the corner of the kitchen, his not-quite-adult cat body pressed into the small space between the end of a cabinet and the wall.

"Nutsy? You OK, honey?" she said softly. "What's the problem?"

Usually after eliminating a hairball—a quite natural occurrence for a cat—Nutsy would play on her sympathy and seek a treat. This time he jerked back from Amy's fingers, eyes wide, his posture almost defensive.

"Nutsy? What's—"

The kitten bolted past the surprised Amy, ignoring her outstretched hand. He raced to his sanctuary under the couch. When Amy crouched down to try to lure him out, she noticed that his body was trembling. She tried to get a hand to him to soothe him. Nutsy backed farther under the couch. She'd never seen her pet act like this. He was, if anything, overly gregarious, a lover of people, and totally devoted to her. *Something's wrong here*, she thought.

She dashed to the telephone in the kitchen, checked Julie's card on her corkboard, and dialed Danny Pulver's clinic number. The vet's recorded voice told her the clinic was closed, gave her the regular hours, and recited a number to call if there was an emergency. Amy scratched the number down on the pad she kept on the counter near the telephone and compared it with Julie's home phone written on the back of the *News-Express* card. The numbers were the same. She dialed quickly, tapping her foot as the phone rang three times before it was answered.

"Dr. Pulver. How can I help you?"

"Doctor, this is Amy Hawkins. I didn't want to bother you at home, but I'm really concerned about my cat."

"Have I seen the cat previously, Amy?" the vet asked.

"No, he's never been sick, and he's only about five months old. He's never acted like this before."

"Tell me what he's doing. And calm down—we'll take care of him. You sound a bit frantic."

"I am. I've never had a cat before and . . . well . . ."

"Sure. I understand. Now, tell me what he's doing."

Amy ran through Nutsy's actions since she'd heard him throwing up, describing his aversion to being touched and the look of panic in his eyes. "His whole body is trembling," she finished.

Dr. Pulver's voice was calm and reassuring. "I don't think there's anything wrong with your kitten, Amy, except for the fact that we're due for some severe weather soon. The swing in the atmospheric pressure affects lots of animals. It frightens them, disorients them. Horses are particularly susceptible, and so are dogs and cats. It's completely natural. It's his instinct telling him to hide, to find a safe place. And he's plain scared. When he's ready to be sociable again, he will be. Until then, I'd leave him alone."

"Are you sure? We've had rain before, and he never had a problem with it."

"There's more than just rain coming. Believe me, your cat's fine. I've had several calls just like yours, and I've told the others just what I'm telling you. Of course, I'll see your cat if you want to meet me at my clinic, but I don't think that's necessary."

Amy calmed a bit. "If you're that certain, Dr. Pulver . . ."

"I am," he assured her. He laughed. "Right at this moment I have eighty pounds of mature collie trying to climb into my lap. My dog, Sunday, isn't afraid of much of anything—except what his instinct tells him to be frightened of."

Amy released a long breath. "Thanks so much, Dr. Pulver. I really do appreciate your time."

"Sure," he said. "That's what I'm here for. Hey, Julie told me she met you the other day. I'm looking forward to doing the same. Please stop by sometime, with or without your cat."

"I'll do that, Dr. Pulver. Please say hi to Julie for me."

"It's Danny, Amy—and I'll tell Julie I talked with you and that you sent your regards."

After thanking the vet again, Julie hung up, feeling infinitely better about what was going on with Nutsy. Danny's words, "When he's ready to be sociable again, he will be," repeated in her mind. The vet's voice and his unhurried, logical, no-nonsense approach to her problem calmed Amy. *Nutsy now has a doctor*, she thought as she returned to her love seat and book. *And I need to get together with Julie—and Maggie too—soon. I don't want our friendships to fade before they have a chance to really get started.*

93

The book didn't hold Amy's attention this time. After a half hour of struggling with it—reading the same paragraph over two and three times—she gave up. Nutsy was still under the couch, and she suspected he was going to be there for a while. She dropped the book at her side and stared across the room through the picture window at the darkness outside. Everything was silent; the night birds she'd gotten used to hearing weren't out tonight, and there was no shushing of the occasional breeze that generally visited on and off at night. The air, Amy noticed, seemed heavy, thicker somehow than normal, although not terribly humid and not at all hot. She was suddenly quite tired, although she'd spent the majority of the day doing nothing more strenuous than reading.

Even though it was barely 9:30, Amy decided to go to bed. She left a lamp near the couch on and stood at it for a few moments, hoping Nutsy would come out to her. He didn't. She sighed and went up the stairs to her room, missing her feline companion already.

It started as rain in the very small hours of the night, when the darkness was the deepest. At first there was no wind behind the rain; it fell straight down from the sky, its liquid, roof-tapping sound barely audible. Amy turned restlessly in her sleep and awakened enough to realize that it was raining. She reached for Nutsy, found his place on her pillow vacant, and pictured the kitten cowering under the couch. Dan Pulver's words returned to her, and she slept again.

By the time the dreary and drenched first light appeared, the wind had started. At first it was light and undecided as to direction. That changed rapidly. By the time Amy got out of bed, the wind was from the west and moving strongly, with gusts that were powerful enough to drive the rain into almost horizontal sheets.

Amy made coffee in her kitchen and stood looking out the window toward the back of her property. Although it was almost 7:00 a.m., there was a late-evening texture to the light. Amy had turned on the overhead and a lamp in the living room as she checked on her cat under the couch. His eyes remained wide, and he ignored her crooning to him and her outstretched finger. She left those lights burning and put both lights on in the kitchen. Still, the darkness was pervasive.

The day was going backward—it should have been becoming lighter, and instead, it was getting progressively darker. The wind whined outside. The rain was more forceful, rattling against her windows and against the siding of her home, like pebbles thrown from spinning tires.

Amy switched on the radio in her living room. The local Coldwater station—the one that offered weather reports every fifteen minutes, along with a female host who was so indomitably perky that she made Amy grind her teeth—was saying, "And no road travel, at least for a few hours. A listener reported a funnel just outside Porterville, but we don't have verification of that as yet. Porterville is, of course, less than sixty miles from Coldwater. Again, people—please don't attempt any sort of travel. Stay inside, and if you have a storm cellar, now is the time to use it. Any livestock that can be gotten safely into a barn or behind a good windbreak should be moved there as soon as possible. But if you have stock in far-flung pastures that'll take some time to get to, leave them be. That's my best advice, folks. All meteorological indications are that this storm is a major weather event. Stay inside and stay safe." There was a moment of static. "I'll keep you up to the minute as to what's happening. Keep your dial right here at . . ."

Amy's house shook for a moment, as if a gigantic hand had struck it. Then the lights went out, the radio died, and the wind escalated to a shrieking howl. She dashed to the kitchen and yanked open a drawer. The flashlight she'd purchased the week she moved into her new home and hadn't yet used cast a bright cone of light through the darkness. Again the entire house seemed to tremble as a massive gust assaulted it. A metal-against-metal screech was even louder than the roar of the wind. The bathroom door upstairs slammed closed, and the impact sounded like a gunshot.

Amy ran up the stairs and pushed open the door. She was struck with a burst of cold, wet air that brought a gasp from her throat. The bathroom window—a casement unit that Amy had left partially cranked open—had been wrenched out of the wall and hurled off into the storm. She looked for a moment at the gaping hole where the window had once been, feeling almost physical pain at the damage to her home. Then, she stepped out of the bathroom and closed the door, feeling the pressure of the wind against it as she did so.

The basement. I need to get to the basement. The house

shivered again, trembling like a creature in pain, as Amy dashed downstairs and into the kitchen. She flicked the beam of her flashlight to the couch: there was no sign of Nutsy. *He's safe enough under there*, she thought. *He'll be fine unless the roof* . . . She stopped the thought, refused to view the image that flashed in her mind.

Amy had her hand on the knob of the door leading to the basement stairs when heavy pounding at the front door battled with the freight-train clamor of the storm. As she turned toward the door, it swung open.

"Come on, Amy," Jake shouted. "Let's get over to my storm cellar—and let's do it now!" A wave of rain pelted the man and spattered against the door and the wall inside the entryway. Jake's face was dripping wet and his jeans soaked. The yellow slicker he wore glistened as Amy directed her light at him. "Come on, Amy!" he urged. "I don't want you here alone."

Amy began to respond but then stopped and pawed through a closet, pulling out a long raincoat that'd probably be next to useless in the furor outside. She hustled down the hallway to Jake, who was still holding the door against the wind that was doing its best to slam the door against the wall. He grabbed her hand and led her outside, shutting the door. His pickup stood in the driveway with its engine running and lights on high beam. The heavy vehicle shuddered as it was hit broadside by a gust, and a sheet of rain obscured the vehicle and even the headlights from view for a moment. Amy's unbuttoned raincoat stood out behind her like a cape, and in a matter of seconds her shirt and jeans were soaked with the chilling, wind-driven squall. She used her hand to protect her eyes from the stinging rain as Jake pulled her off the porch and to his truck.

He leaned close to her and shouted into her ear, "I'll open the door, and you jump in. If I let the door go, the wind'll tear it off. Ready?"

Amy nodded, not trusting her voice. Jake braced his body against the door, and Amy scrambled into the cab of the pickup, followed by a torrent of rain. The door slammed next to her with an impact that moved the entire vehicle. Jake, barely a shadow in the downpour, crossed in front of the hood and backed into the driver's seat, both hands holding the door against the wind. "You OK?" he asked in the relative quiet of the truck interior.

She nodded. "Yes. I've never seen anything like . . ." Her voice died out.

"I figured your first storm would be kind of rough on you, Amy. My storm cellar has light—I have a gasoline generator—and food and water." He grinned. "All the comforts of home." She wondered how Jake was able to drive. Even with the high beams on, Amy couldn't see more than a few feet beyond the front of the truck—and even then, the rain pounded so hard at times she couldn't see at all.

Jake's hands grasped the steering wheel at the top, and his knuckles showed pale in the half-light. He rolled ahead in first gear, playing with the clutch, steering into the power of gusts, doing his best to stay on the road.

When the headlamps prodded the side of Jake's house, Amy breathed a long sigh of relief.

"I know what you mean," Jake said. "About half the time, I couldn't see a thing. Stay here—I'll go around and open your door, just like I did at your place."

The temperature in the cab seemed to drop twenty degrees as Jake opened his door, slid out, and let the wind slam the door behind him. In a moment he rapped on the window next to Amy and began opening her door. He waited out a long, howling gust and then tugged the door open just wide enough for Amy to climb out. "Hold on to me," he shouted at her. He didn't have to ask twice; the force of the wind felt like it would carry Amy off and whirl her into the sky, never to be seen again. She locked her hands onto Jake's slicker. He clutched her forearm with a strong, reassuring hand and began walking, guiding her along with him.

There were four concrete steps that led downward to a heavy wooden door that was well below grade. Jake hauled the door open and tugged Amy inside, leaving much of the cacophony of the storm outside. Light—seeming terribly bright after the dark—filled the storm cellar and flowed from three bulbs suspended from the ceiling. There were three steel floor jacks positioned around the room, and one at each corner. Crude shelves held canned food and large clear glass jugs of water. A coffeepot perked on a heating coil on a card table. On a ratty-looking couch Mallory Powers sat wrapped in a blanket, a fresh abrasion on her forehead, her right leg extended straight out, and her ankle wrapped heavily with an Ace bandage.

"Mal was running a few head of horses into the warehouse arena when the wind caught the door and slammed it against her leg and ankle," Jake explained. "Knocked her right off her horse."

"That's awful. I'm so sorry," Amy said. "Is there anything I can do for you?"

Mallory shook her head. "I'm OK."

"Look, I've got to give the boys a hand with the horses. There're a bunch of towels in the bathroom," Jake said, motioning toward a closed door. "Dry yourself off as well as you can. Have some coffee. I'll be back soon."

The storm shrieked as Jake opened the door and slipped out, and then the storm cellar returned to semi-silence. "Can I get you some coffee, Mallory?" Amy asked.

"No thanks," she mumbled.

"Are you sure? It's no bother."

"Look, this is nothing. I banged my foot a bit, is all. I'd still be out there helping the guys if Jake hadn't made such a big deal out of it. You don't need to start playing little miss nursemaid." Her voice was hard and sharp, and when Amy looked into her eyes, the fire there was disturbing.

"I'm not playing nursemaid. I just thought . . ."

"If I need anything, I'll ask for it, OK?"

What in the world? Amy thought. *All I did was offer to fix her a cup of coffee. What's with her and her attitude? Is she in shock or something?*

Amy went into the tiny bathroom and found a stack of towels and dried her hair as best she could. Her jeans and shirt remained wet, and there was nothing she could do about that right then. The coffee—raw and hot and overly strong—tasted wonderful. She sipped and then sipped again, letting the liquid warm her.

Mallory shifted her position on the couch and pulled the blanket a little more tightly around herself. Amy met the other woman's eyes for a moment and then looked away. A silence built in the room, punctuated only occasionally by the creaking and groaning of the house above them. It was an uneasy quiet, at least for Amy. After several long minutes, she said, "What is it about me that bothers you, Mallory? Because there must be something. If I've upset you somehow, I didn't mean to do it. Ever since we met, you've seemed to take a dislike to me. I don't understand it."

Mal's voice was mocking. "You don't understand it? Maybe things are a lot different in New York City, but out here in the boonies we don't fall all over other women's men."

Surprise took Amy's voice for a moment. "What are you talking about?" she demanded.

"Like you don't have any idea what I mean, right?" Mallory sneered. "You haven't been leading Jake on with your big-time city guile, I suppose? Your oh-so-important book?"

It was as if Amy had been struck physically and unexpectedly. Her mind reeled as she attempted to process what she was hearing and the wrath that was so obvious in Mallory Powers. She took a breath and hoped that her voice wouldn't quiver as she spoke. "I'm really sorry you feel that way. But I need to say that I haven't been chasing Jake."

Mallory's eyes glistened. She spoke as if she hadn't heard what Amy had said. "I suppose you didn't know how Jake feels about me—about the plans he has for us."

Amy struggled against the anger that was rising inside her. She waited a heartbeat. "You've made your opinion known."

Mallory's smile was patently false. "I sure have."

Amy took a deep breath and tried to reason with Mallory once again. "This whole thing is silly. The storm and you getting hurt has put all of our nerves on edge. Let's try to—"

"I meant every word I said." The tremor of tension was clear in Mallory's voice. "I don't have the fancy college degrees you have, but I've forgotten more about horses and ranching than you'll ever know, and it's that sort of thing that's important to Jake Winter."

Amy sighed loudly. "Fancy degrees? Lots of English majors with master's degrees are slinging hamburgers and clerking in department stores. But all this animosity toward me isn't going to accomplish a thing."

"We'll see about—" Mallory's response was cut off by the opening of the door to the exterior and the sudden scream of the wind outside. Jake entered the room, water streaming from his hair, his yellow slicker already creating a puddle where he stood. "All the horses are in the arena, and the boys are looking after them," he said. He grinned at Mallory and then turned his smile toward Amy. "The storm isn't all bad. At least you ladies had the opportunity for a nice talk," he said.

If there hadn't been so much tension in the room, Amy would have laughed out loud.

The storm lost its teeth by midafternoon. A few widespread tornadoes were reported, but none had struck inhabited areas. When Amy stepped up the concrete stairs and out into Jake's side yard, the air was fresh, cool, wonderfully clean. She inhaled deeply, relishing the purity, particularly after several hours in the storm cellar. Behind her, Jake helped Mallory hobble-hop up the steps with his arm around her waist. Mal attempted to support her weight on her injured foot and lurched sideways, yelping in pain. Her right arm clutched at Jake's body.

Jake and Mallory shuffled unsteadily to the travel trailer. Amy stood where she was, marveling at the just-scoured appearance of everything around her. Jake's grass sparkled with a springlike luster, washed free of dust that'd accumulated during the dry spell. The fencing around the nearest paddock looked freshly painted; Amy had never seen it free of the grit that dulled its whiteness.

Jake came up behind her. "Everything looks good after a storm, doesn't it?"

Amy nodded. "It's more striking here than in New York. There, it's pretty much only the streets that look clean. Here, it's everything."

"Smells great too," Jake said. "C'mon, Amy, I'll run you home, and we can check your place for damage." They started toward Jake's pickup.

"My bathroom window was blown out and away. Other than that, I'm hoping everything's OK—and that my cat has recovered."

Jake guided Amy to the passenger door. "I know a good carpenter to reinstall a window for you. I'll give him a call from your place."

"I'd appreciate that. I don't like the idea of having that huge hole in my wall any longer than I have to."

Jake started his engine, turned the truck around, and drove down the driveway to the road. "What did you and Mal talk about?" he asked. "Did she bend your ear about her training work?"

"Well . . . no," Amy answered carefully. "We didn't get into horses at all."

Jake nodded and dropped the subject, making it obvious that his question had been a matter of polite conversation, not curiosity.

"Interesting lady," Amy said without expanding the idea.

Jake turned into Amy's driveway. "Sure," he said noncommittally. "Let's take a look at your bathroom."

Nutsy charged Amy the moment she stepped in the front door. He was already purring and mewing loudly.

"Seems like your cat did just fine," Jake observed. "If he purred any louder, we'd need earplugs."

Amy scooped the kitten up from the floor and cradled him against her chest. She led Jake to the bathroom as she scratched Nutsy's chin and rubbed behind his ears.

Jake observed the gaping hole. "You'll need a whole new frame," he said. "No big deal, though. Ben Callan—that's my friend's name—will make it look like new."

Jake made the call from Amy's kitchen and left a message on the carpenter's recorder. Then he and Amy faced one another, Amy still holding Nutsy. "Thanks for thinking of me, Jake. I appreciate it. I'll admit I was scared."

Jake smiled. "I'll let you in on a little secret, Amy," he said. "Anyone with more sense than a hedgehog is a little scared during a storm like that."

"That's good to know, I guess," Amy said. "Anyway, it's good to have you for a neighbor."

The moment became self-conscious then. Jake looked like he had more to say, and his blush indicated he was having trouble putting whatever it was into words. Amy broke the tension for him by speaking. "Thanks again for all your help."

"Glad to help out. Well, I better get going. I have things that need doing—like checking my fences. I'll see you soon, Amy," he said and turned to the door.

Was it something about Mallory he wanted to tell me? Amy wondered. *Or was he in a hurry to see if he had storm damage? It's hard to tell what's on these cowboys' minds. I'm sure glad he came after me, though. The thought of waiting out that storm here, alone . . . Even with Mallory's nonsense, I'm glad I was there rather than here.*

Amy dumped Nutsy's old kibble, although it was perfectly edible, and gave him a new bowlful. She freshened his water and then stood at the window over her sink, looking out over her land.

That she felt some attraction to Jake Winter wasn't a surprise. *But the last thing I need right now is to get in the middle of some crazy triangle with Jake and Mallory.* She put relationships and her book and the storm out of her mind and concentrated on scratching and playing with Nutsy.

Amy walked into the living room and turned off the

overhead light that had come on when the power was restored. Her jeans were still wet; she didn't want to sit on her couch. The idea of dry clothing sounded awfully good, and she headed for her room. As she changed, her stomach grumbled at her loudly, and she realized how hungry she was. A quick picture of one of Jake's burgers or a meal at Drago's Café flashed in her mind, generating a rush of saliva in her mouth.

"Not tonight," she said aloud. "It's canned soup and a toasted cheese sandwich. I've had enough adventure for one day."

5

Morning brought the glorious sort of day that Amy had grown to love in Montana.

There was a sweet and gentle breeze, the sun was barely beginning to assert its strength, and the air outside was as fragrant and promising as it was in Amy's kitchen—where her first pot of coffee was gurgling happily. When the doorbell rang she looked up at the clock: 7:22. She set her still-empty mug on the counter and went to the front of her house. The peephole in her door showed a tall, rather thin man about Amy's age—thirty-five or so—wearing jeans and a flannel shirt with the sleeves rolled up over hard, muscular forearms. His hair—dark brown with some strands of gray—was moderately long, and he wore a scruffy-looking mustache. Amy's hand rested on the doorknob as she decided whether to open the door without verifying who the fellow was. He must have caught her movement behind the peephole.

"I'm Ben Callan," he said. "Jake Winter called yesterday and said if I didn't get here early today, he'd nail my hide to the front door of his barn."

Amy laughed and opened the door. "You're just in time for coffee, Ben," she said. She extended her hand. "I'm Amy Hawkins. I really appreciate your coming out on a Saturday morning like this."

Ben's smile was broad. "Can't have a friend of Jake's goin' without a window, now, can we?" His voice was a distinctive one, fairly deep in tone but quiet, with clear, slightly softened vowels—a Montana voice. "I'll tell you what," he went on, "let me measure the space and call the supply yard to send over the frame an' window and then I'll take you up on that coffee you mentioned. If it's no trouble, I mean."

"No trouble at all," Amy said. "The bathroom's right at the end of the stairs, on the left. Come on to the kitchen after you get your measurements."

When the carpenter strode into the kitchen not five minutes later, he smiled at Amy again. "You're in luck. Your window's a common size. If I can use your phone, I'll see how quick I can get one for you."

Amy pointed toward the wall, indicating her telephone. "I hope it's not a long wait. I'd hate to have to board up the only window in my bathroom."

Ben began to dial. "Shouldn't be a problem. Like I said, it's a common size." Then he spoke into the phone. "Jimmy? Ben Callan. Look, I'm on an emergency job, and I need an Anderson casement window." He consulted the scrap of paper in his other hand and read the specifications. "How soon can you get one to me?" He gave Amy's address and then laughed and turned to Amy, winking at her. "Great, Jim. I appreciate it. Thanks."

Ben hung up, looking quite satisfied with the results of the call. "The yard will have the whole kit an' caboodle here in a half hour or so. Won't take me long to fit the window and repair the damage and the siding."

"Wonderful." Amy motioned to the kitchen table. "Have a seat."

The man hesitated. "Well, I was kinda wondering if we couldn't take our coffee outside. I've got a new puppy in my truck, and I'd like to let him out to play a bit. OK with you?"

Amy handed Ben a filled and steaming mug. She'd stop asking Montana men how they took their coffee. There seemed to be a state law against milk or sugar, at least with the male gender. *See? I'm learning to fit in.* "Let's go. I'd love to see your puppy."

Ben looked into his mug and then up into Amy's eyes. "You wouldn't have a touch of milk an' maybe a spoonful of sugar handy, would you?"

When Amy broke into laughter, he looked at her curiously. "It's nothing, Ben," she explained. "I just thought of something funny."

"Oh? What?"

"I was just praising myself for knowing that Montana guys don't take anything in their coffee—and then you asked for milk and sugar."

Ben laughed. "Maybe it's just the cowboys like Jake who drink it black. I don't even own a horse—and to tell you the truth, I can't say that I care to either. We contractors and handymen take milk and sugar."

Amy led the way to the door, and they walked out to the driveway. She caught her breath as Ben swung open the door of his pickup and a five- or six-month-old collie jumped easily to the ground and stood for a moment, looking around himself, obviously curious about the new surroundings.

"He's gorgeous," Amy said.

"I won't argue with you about that. Danny Pulver—Doc Pulver, the vet—owns my pup's daddy. Danny's collie, Sunday, well, you couldn't find a better bloodline."

"What's your pup's name?"

"Zack," Ben said. "After my last dog. See, I had another name for the pup, but I kept calling him Zack out of habit, and then decided it was kind of a memorial to ol' Zack if I let the little guy have his name. My original Zack died of old age six months ago. He was a great ol' dog, and my new Zack is just like him."

Amy grinned. The love Ben showed for both his dogs made her feel good, and his pride in his new pup was as obvious as his smile.

Ben whistled a short note and then called, "Zack, come on over here and meet Amy."

The dog was striking. Zack was leggy, as collies always are at that age, and his chest was full and his head noble. His muzzle was straight and his eyes well set. His ears tuliped over at the tip like those of the collies in the winner's circle at the Westminster Dog Show. His coat was a deeply burnished brass hue, and the white bib and forepaws were as bright as fresh snow. Zack trotted over to Ben and stood

PAIGE LEE ELLISTON

looking up at the man, and his plumed tail moved slowly back and forth.

Amy crouched and beckoned to the young dog. Zack stepped to her, and she rubbed behind his ears and stroked his neck. "If you ever need a puppy-sitter," she told Ben, "give me a call. And that's not just a polite offer—I mean it." She held the pup's head between her hands. "I'd love to have a dog like this."

"I'll definitely keep that in mind, Amy. Thing is, Zack goes pretty much everywhere with me, but if the occasion comes up, you'll be the one I call." He paused. "Have you ever thought of getting a dog of your own? It's real clear that you love them—and look how Zack's taking to you."

"That's a good question," Amy admitted. "I guess I haven't given much thought to getting a pup—at least not until I met Zack, here. He's got me thinking."

That seemed to please Ben. "A good dog will add a lot to a person's life," he said. He looked out toward the road, where a pickup was slowing and then beginning the turn in Amy's driveway. "Ol' Jimmy's right on the ball this morning with his deliveries. There's your window," he said.

Amy played with Zack while the carpenter worked. She was fascinated by the puppy—his intelligence, his quick acceptance of her as a friend, his intense curiosity about every new sight and scent he discovered. By the time Ben was finished installing the window and repairing the wind damage, Amy knew she'd find it hard to say good-bye to Zack.

111

"What do I owe you?" she asked Ben as they stood near his truck. "I'll go inside and write you a check."

"I didn't get any paperwork with the window unit, so I'll need to check with the yard. I'll do that and get an invoice in the mail to you. OK?"

"Fine. And thanks, Ben."

"Sure." He looked into Amy's eyes, and they held the gaze for a moment. She hadn't really noticed Ben's eyes before. Now, she saw that they were a rich and deep chestnut and that they were warm and inviting. "Maybe I could come by again—with Zack, I mean. If you'd like." After an awkward moment, he added rather clumsily, "If it's OK with you, I mean."

"I'd like that a lot," Amy said. "Please do."

Ben opened his pickup door and motioned the pup inside. Zack settled himself in the passenger seat and then looked out through the windshield at Amy. Ben started the truck and began backing down the driveway. Amy raised her hand to wave. *Am I waving to the dog or to the guy?*

Later that day, the fun Amy had with the collie pup and the relief she felt at having her window and wall repaired dwindled away. She felt adrift, somehow, and quite alone. She wandered to her reading chair and finished the book she'd been reading. Then she set it carefully aside and gazed out through her picture window. The silence that she generally cherished seemed to deepen until it became almost funereal. Nutsy slept peacefully on the couch, and for a moment she envied the kitten. *The biggest thing he needs to worry about is whether or not he can maneuver another treat out of me. Not a bad life.*

Amy stood, consciously attempting to chase away the low-key sensation that was trying to settle over her. "Julie," she said aloud, startling Nutsy. "Julie said call anytime. How about right now?" She hurried to the phone in the kitchen and dialed Julie's number.

"Hello, this is Julie."

"Hi, Julie, it's Amy Hawkins." She tried to force some lightness into her voice. "I just called to say hey and to see what you're up to."

"Amy! Good to hear from you. You get through the storm OK?"

"Pretty much. I left a window partially open, though, and the wind tore the whole thing off. Ben Callan was here to replace it."

"Ben always does a good job. Hey, what're you doing right now? Danny is off to a veterinary convention in Butte until tomorrow, and I'm about to go stir-crazy just sitting around alone. Why don't you come over?"

"I'd love to."

"Good! See you in a few minutes, then. You know where our place is?"

"Sure. I've driven past it a few times. See you in a few!"

Amy felt her spirits lifting as soon as she climbed into her Jeep and keyed the engine. It'd been a good day so far. Spending time with Julie would make it even better. *My window's fixed, and Ben Callan and Zack . . .*

She pictured the pup in her mind again as she drove

to Julie's home. The collie's quick yip of excitement as she threw the ragged and well-chewed softball Ben had provided, the dog's obvious pride in returning the ball to Amy and dropping it at her feet, the silky-warm texture of his coat, brought a fond smile to her face. *I'll look in to getting a dog*, she promised herself. *There shouldn't be a problem with Nutsy—kittens and pups get along with one another just fine when they're introduced at a young age.* In her mind she saw Ben smiling at her and asking for milk and sugar for his coffee. *I hope he does stop by. There's something about him . . .*

Julie's home was as Amy remembered it: an older, rehabbed farmhouse with a small barn situated to the rear and long lines of wooden fencing enclosing lush green pasture. There was a horse trailer parked next to the barn, and a small tractor—larger than a suburban lawn tractor but smaller than the big farming machines—was hooked to a flatbed-type wagon on the opposite side of the barn. The entire place gave the impression of neatness and order, and the two horses grazing in a paddock not far from the house completed the image of Montana harmony.

Amy parked behind Julie's pickup, and as she stepped out of her Jeep a large collie trotted over from the house and stood facing her, not barking but, she thought, appraising her. In a moment Julie followed, looking fresh in jeans, boots, and a flannel shirt. "Don't mind Sunday," she called to Amy. "He was hoping Danny was with you."

Amy crouched and held her hand out to the dog. He sniffed it, and his tail wagged. "He's the second wonderful

114

collie I've met today," Amy said. "Ben Callan brought his Zack along when he fixed my window this morning."

"Sunday's Zack's father, you know," Julie said. "He's a terrific pup. From what I heard, there's only one left from the litter of six that hasn't gone to a home. Danny doesn't ordinarily breed Sunday, but the female is the sweetest dog ever, and we all thought they'd bring some great youngsters into the world."

Amy stood and faced Julie, smiling. Neither woman moved toward the embrace that was so common in the cities Amy was used to and so rare in rural Montana. Those quick and showy hugs and the ridiculous air-kisses Amy had watched and experienced so many times were, in her opinion, part of a much different society—one predicated on image rather than substance, outward flash rather than friendship.

"C'mon," Julie said, "I'll show you through the barn, and then we'll go inside and visit."

The barn, like the rest of the property, was clean and neat, with the cement floor litter-free and various pieces of horse equipment hung from walls and arranged on shelves. Two Western saddles rested on sawhorse-type racks. Amy took a long draught of air: the scents of polished leather, straw, hay, wood, and the molasses of the grain in the feed barrels combined in a wave of what Amy was coming to recognize as the perfume of Montana.

"Smells good, doesn't it?" Julie said. "It's something I've never tired of."

Amy nodded. "It's kind of a symbol for me," she said. "I've

been in a few barns since I've been in Coldwater, and this freshness—this wonderful smell—is Montana to me."

Julie laughed. "I can see why you're the novelist and I'm a news writer. Let's go have some coffee. I've got cookies from the bakery in town too."

"Empty-calorie type with too much sugar?" Amy asked.

"You betcha! Frosted too."

"Perfect!"

The conversation moved easily between the two women. They laughed together as they discussed inconsequentials, commiserated over grocery prices, and found that they both read many of the same fiction writers.

"How's your novel coming?" Julie asked.

The smile left Amy's face. She hesitated a moment before speaking. "That's a problem. It isn't going terribly well."

"Oh? Why's that?"

"I'm not sure." She was silent for a moment. "It's a temporary thing; no big deal. I'll get back into it soon." She paused again.

"Sounds a little scary."

"Well . . . yeah," Amy admitted. "Or, maybe more frustrating than scary."

Julie nodded. "I've had bad days and lazy days at writing, but those things were gone after a night's sleep." She stood from the armchair she sat in and walked to Amy on the couch. She took Amy's empty cup from the coffee table. "I suppose all you can do is not let it get the best of you."

Amy's smile was a bit forced. "I won't."

Julie took the empty cups to the kitchen. Amy looked at the framed Frederic Remington reprints on the wall. Neither was the same work that hung in Jake Winter's living room. There was a finely crafted Indian blanket displayed as a wall hanging, its colors vivid, the symbols sharp and distinct. She remembered a meeting about an editing job with a bestselling writer in his apartment. On the largest wall he had an original Monet. Amy decided she liked Remington reprints and Crow blankets better. *And I like Julie a world more than I liked that pretentious, self-aggrandizing jerk of a writer or any of the people he hung out with.*

Julie came out of the kitchen with cups of fresh coffee in her hands and Sunday at her heels. She put Amy's cup on the coffee table and sat, once again, in the armchair. Sunday settled down in front of her.

"He's sure loyal," Amy observed.

"He's a wonderful dog, but the only person in his heart is Danny. Sunday likes me well enough, and when Danny's not around, he sticks fairly close to me. But, he's 100 percent Danny's dog."

Amy sipped at her coffee. *Must be great for Danny*, she thought, *being loved to that degree by such a fine animal. Sometime . . . well, anyway, I have Nutsy.*

"We saw your neighbor the other night," Julie said. "Jake. He came over to talk with Danny about being the on-site vet at a rodeo Jake's providing stock for in Porterville."

"Is Danny going to do it?"

"He can't—and he loves rodeo. He's sorry to miss it. But,

he has an old friend from Cornell coming to visit the same weekend."

Julie met Amy's eyes over the rim of her cup. "Jake talked our ears off about your cookouts and his mares digging up your lawn. He says—and this is a direct quote—'I don't think I've met a lady like her before.'"

Amy's blush was followed quickly by a smile. "That's good to hear," she admitted. "He's so different from the men I've been around for the past several years."

"Different how?" Julie asked.

"Different better. There isn't a phony bone in Jake Winter's body. What you see is what you get—and what you see isn't half bad," she added, laughing.

"No, it sure isn't," Julie agreed. She smiled. "Is it possible that you're the least bit smitten with your next-door neighbor?"

Amy blushed again. It wasn't necessary for her to answer. Julie laughed, and then Amy joined her.

Later, as Julie walked Amy to her Jeep, both women stopped to gaze up at the sky. The stars were polished diamonds tossed by a careless hand on a vast field of black velvet. "I'm still amazed at the sky in Montana," Amy said. "I've never seen anything like it before. Those stars—if I had a stepladder, I could touch them."

Julie nodded. "The Lakotas say there's a peak in the Beartooth Mountains that only Indians can see, and that it's so high a person can step from the top of it directly onto the moon and hold the stars in his arms."

"That's not so hard to believe on a night like this," Amy

118

said. "Thanks for a fun visit, Julie. I really enjoyed our time together. I needed it too."

"I enjoyed it too, Amy. Don't be a stranger now, OK? And good luck with the book. I'll pray for you."

Amy carried the warmth of the Pulver home through the night to her own place.

No matter what, I've made the right decision in moving here. She stood outside her garage for another long look into the sky. Although it was after ten o'clock, she didn't feel quite ready for bed. *Too much coffee?* She sat on her porch step, enjoying the silence—which was broken by the grumble of a pair of large stock carrier trucks turning from the road into Jake's driveway. They were white shapes in the distance, but Amy could make out the Winter Rodeo Stock logo—a cowboy on a high bucking horse—when the lights of the second truck splashed on the side of the first. Voices but no words carried to her. She strained to see if Jake was one of the men talking but couldn't tell.

Jake talks about me to his friends. She smiled as she recalled her conversation with Julie. *Am I smitten with Jake Winter? I hardly know the man. I've only been with him a few times. Even so, I find myself thinking about him. Maybe I've been alone a bit too long.*

The engines of the trucks at Jake's shut down, and in a few minutes there were no more voices reaching her. A horse in the pasture closest to her snorted, and as if in answer, so did a couple of others. After a few moments the horses, too, were silent.

Nutsy, mewing and writhing between her ankles, greeted

Amy as she came in the front door. She quickly checked the cat's water and food bowls and then headed up the stairs to bed, very pleased she'd picked up the telephone to call Julie.

The morning came quickly, but it wasn't the light flooding through her curtains that brought Amy from sleep. *Was that the doorbell?* She heard the sound of a vehicle in her driveway and swung her legs from her bed. She scurried to her window just in time to see Ben Callan's pickup halfway down the driveway, headed out toward the road. She looked at her bedside clock radio and yawned. "Ten after six is a little early to come calling on a neighbor, Ben," she said aloud. She watched as the truck swung onto the road and accelerated back toward his home. *What in the world?* she wondered. *Maybe he forgot a tool or something yesterday and needed it for his next job. I wish I'd been up when he came.*

Nutsy went into his morning routine of yowling for a meal. He sounded as if he hadn't been fed in weeks. "I hear you, honey," Amy said as she scratched the kitten's back. "Let me grab a shower and I'll feed you." As if he understood her words, Nutsy jumped back onto the bed and curled up next to Amy's pillow, apparently satisfied to wait for his breakfast.

Downstairs, fresh from her shower, Amy fed the cat and started her Mr. Coffee. The picture of Ben's truck pulling down her driveway replayed in her mind. *Did he drop something off? His invoice? Some kind of a spare part for the window?* She checked her coffee—not quite gurgled out yet—and walked to the front of her house. She opened the front door—and gasped in surprise.

At first she thought it was Zack, Ben's pup. But what would Zack be doing gnawing on a knuckle bone, with a lead from his collar looped over her doorknob? The pup looked up at her, his eyes unsure for a moment. When he saw her smile, his tail wagged. Amy's breath came hard for some reason—and for some reason, tears of happiness sprang to her eyes.

Amy had fallen instantaneously, completely, and unalterably in love.

She crouched next to the puppy and ran her hands along the side of his head, gently, as if touching a baby. His tongue, a rough pink slab that seemed too large for a small dog, licked at her hand. She continued stroking the pup with one hand and picked up the folded sheet of typing paper that was tucked partially under the blanket with the other. The pencil-scrawled note said, "Dear Amy, your heart was in your eyes as you played with Zack. This little guy is the last of the litter and was getting lonely. You need a good dog on your place. Enjoy him. See you soon. Ben."

Amy sat awkwardly next to the basket and hefted the pup into her arms and against her chest. His tongue found her cheek, and she could smell his sweet kibble-and-milk puppy breath and feel his steady heartbeat against her own body. The pup lapped at her nose.

Amy rose, set the pup on his feet next to the basket, and took the end of the leash from around the doorknob. She pushed open the door and said, "C'mon, little guy. Let's go into your new home." She moved away, taking a pair of backward steps. The collie followed her as if he'd been doing so all his life. Nutsy dashed up to the dog; the kitten's fur along his spine stood on end, and his body raised and arced. The pup leaned forward and licked Nutsy's head, ruffling the fur, standing it up, wetting it slightly. Nutsy leaped back, stood assessing the dog for a long moment, and then came ahead, poking his nose against that of the dog. The two traded scents as if they were shaking hands. The collie licked the cat again.

And that quickly, they were friends.

Amy's hand trembled as she took out her Coldwater directory and looked up Ben's number. "He's beautiful—he's wonderful," she babbled as soon as the phone at the other end was picked up. "I don't know how to thank you. This is the sweetest thing that's ever happened to me—the most wondrous gift I've ever received. I . . . you're . . . I just don't know what to say. I'm just flabbergasted, Ben, I can't begin to—"

There was a chuckle. "This here's Hollis Callan, ma'am—Ben's pa. He's just pullin' in the driveway. Want me to fetch him to the phone?" He laughed again. "I guess you like the puppy?"

Amy was too enthralled to be embarrassed. "That's an understatement, Mr. Callan. And I would like to speak to Ben, thank you."

The telephone clattered against a hard surface, and Amy heard footsteps going away from it. In a moment, she heard more steps coming toward it.

"My dad's of the opinion that you like the pup," Ben said.

"Like him? Ben, he's perfect. I love him to pieces. I don't know how to thank you."

"A country lady needs a good ol' dog." Ben chuckled. "I felt almost guilty driving away with Zack yesterday, taking him away from you. So, I knew that there was only the one pup left, and, well, I knew where his home was." He paused. "What are you going to name him?"

"Oh, I . . . I haven't given that a thought. Any ideas?"

"Seems to me the best way to come up with a name is to watch a new animal, see how he acts, how he plays, what he's afraid of. I think that pup will name himself." He laughed. "I just hope you don't have to call him Puddles."

"He's bright," Amy said. "He'll be easy to housebreak."

Ben laughed again.

"What?" Amy asked.

"You've owned the dog for fifteen minutes and you already know how smart he is?"

"Well, I could be a little prejudiced in his favor," she admitted.

"You're supposed to be."

She hesitated a moment. "Hey, I've got to go to town and pick up some puppy chow at the grocery store. I can pick up a couple of steaks too. Can you come for dinner tonight?"

"I'd love to, Amy. What can I bring?"

"Not a thing—you already brought something wonderful today."

Amy unboxed the new Weber grill she'd bought in Coldwater and placed it behind her garage. The pup had ridden in her Jeep on the passenger seat fearfully, hesitantly, for the first few minutes. Then, when he discovered he could stick his muzzle out the partially lowered window, he began to enjoy the trip.

The rectangular cedar picnic table that hadn't yet made it out of the garage was awkward to handle, but Amy was able to muscle it out to the backyard, near the grill. She put a lawn chair on either side of the table and settled in one to watch her puppy play in the grass. He was fascinated with the grasshoppers and the other insects that lived in the lawn; he chased them, pounced on them, and ate them. She called to the dog when he'd wandered a bit too far from where she sat, and he ran back to her in the slightly clumsy gallop of a puppy. She praised him lavishly for obeying her call. The pup sat at her feet looking up at her, his eyes showing that he was almost impossibly happy that he had pleased his new mistress.

The collie's face triggered a memory, and Amy struggled to recover it from her childhood. Slowly it became clear: the cover of a hardcover book, a gift for her tenth birthday. It was a novel about a collie by Albert Payson Terhune, and the dog's name was Bobby, respectfully named after the Scottish poet Robert Burns. Something clicked into place in Amy's heart. She'd loved the novel, and it had led her to the exploration of Burns's poetry. "Bobby," she whispered to the puppy. And, from that moment forward, his name was Bobby.

One of the toys Amy had bought for Bobby in the Coldwater grocery store was a rawhide knot the size of a baseball. The pup fell in love with the toy immediately. Amy tossed it around the yard for Bobby to fetch, and both of them relished the simple game. Later in the afternoon she watched the pup as he slept in his basket, tired from his day of play. Nutsy approached Bobby cautiously, watched for a while, and then climbed into the basket, pressing himself against Bobby's side for his own late-day doze. The pup's sleep was deep, and every so often his feet twitched, as if he were running in a dream. *Probably chasing his rawhide knot*, Amy thought.

Bobby has already added so much to my life. For Ben to realize how happy a puppy would make me and then to put everything in motion was so kind, so sweet. I hope that one day I can do something for someone else that means as much to them as Bobby means to me.

Amy was in the backyard when Ben's truck pulled into her driveway and stopped behind her Jeep. She cut through the garage and rushed up to the man, wrapping him in a quick embrace. Ben was startled by the hug—and Amy was a little bit as well.

"I'm so thankful to you for Bobby."

Ben's arm tightened slightly, comfortably, around Amy's shoulders for a brief moment before she stepped back. He smelled of Ivory soap, she noticed, and his hair of shampoo. "Bobby?" he asked.

"After the poet, Robert Burns," Amy explained. "He's Scottish, and so are collies, so . . ."

"Wee sleekit timrous cowerin' mousie," Ben recited.

"You know Burns's poetry?" Amy laughed delightedly. The line from one of her favorites sounded strange when articulated with a Western drawl rather than a Scottish burr.

"No, not really, but I had a grammar school teacher, Mrs. MacPherson, who was obsessed with him. She read to us from his collected poems daily." Ben reached into his truck and brought out a quart of Ben and Jerry's Cherry Garcia. "I brought some dessert," he said. He handed it to Amy.

"You go out back, and I'll put the ice cream away and bring us a drink. Would you like iced tea? Diet Pepsi? Coffee?"

"Iced tea sounds good." He sniffed the air. "I see you've got the fire going already."

"I wanted it to be perfect for the steaks," Amy answered. She started to the house, stopped in midstride, and turned back to Ben. "Hey, where's Zack?"

"With my dad. He loves Zack as much as I do. I couldn't say no to him."

"Well, I'm sure Zack's heart is more than big enough to share with the both of you. I was looking forward to seeing him, though. It would have been fun watching the two pups play together."

"Next time," Ben said. It was a statement, not a question.

"For sure," Amy said. She turned back to the kitchen, Bobby at her heels. "Go on and sit down, Ben. I'll be out in a minute." *Next time? That kind of answers the question*

126

if we'll get together again, doesn't it? The thought brought a smile to her face.

The steaks—prime sirloins Amy had overspent on because of the occasion—were excellent. The conversation moved from Bobby to the food to the weather to other topics and then back to Bobby.

"I don't even know if there are leash laws in this area," Amy admitted.

"There aren't," Ben told her, "but Bobby needs to have a yearly rabies inoculation. Doc Pulver can take care of that for you." He added, "I'm assuming you're going to use Danny as your vet."

"Yep, I am. No doubt about that. I wouldn't be able to face Julie again if I took Bobby anywhere else."

"And, there's the point that Danny's the best vet within a hundred miles of us."

After their meal they sipped their coffee and watched the colors in the western sky as the sun began its downward swing. They were comfortable together, at ease, learning things about one another. Amy liked the way all that felt.

"How long have you been in business for yourself, Ben?" she asked.

"Going on a dozen years now. It was Callan & Son from the time I got out of the army until then. I was working with my dad. He had a stroke. It was a mild enough stroke—or so the doctors said—but it ended his carpentry days. I took over the business from him."

"He sounded pretty good when I spoke with him this morning. Happy enough, anyway."

"Oh, he's in pretty decent shape. And as feisty as an ol' rooster. He doesn't have too much use of the left side of his body, but he uses a walker and gets around OK. He's always after me to leave the handyman stuff behind and go into furniture and cabinetmaking. Some day, I'll do just that, but right now, well, the bills need to be paid."

"Do you do any furniture making now? I was in a couple of shops in Massachusetts a few years ago and was fascinated by what those guys could do. It's a real art form, isn't it?"

"Yeah. It is when it's done right. I take a contract every so often to build a hutch or a table or whatever. I really love it, and if I thought I could support my dad and me on what I'd make doing it, I'd hang out a shingle tomorrow morning." He drank some coffee. "What about you, Amy? I know you're a writer. From what I've read, that's a hard way to go—all kinds of competition, hard to find a publisher, all that."

"It can be tough at times," Amy said. "I guess I feel about fiction writing like you do about making furniture, though. I love it. It has its ups and downs, and you're right, the competition is always intense. But I still love it."

"It's good to see someone making a living doing something that's really important to him." After a half second, Ben added, "Or her."

Amy laughed. "That 'making a living' part is up for grabs, I'm afraid. I'm about halfway through a novel right now."

"Is it sold already? Is that how it works? Or when it's finished, do you need to show it around to publishers?"

"I'm on a contract to finish the book, and I've gotten an

advance against the royalties we hope it'll generate when it's published."

"I see." He thought for a moment. "It must feel good at the end of a day to see the pile of pages you've written."

Amy couldn't help laughing. "Pile of pages? For most writers four or five good pages are a day's work. That's not much of a pile."

"Hmmm. It sounds like writing a book takes about as long as it takes to make and finish a really fine hutch or sideboard, then. In either case, it's a labor of love, though. Maybe that's what makes each of them worthwhile."

There'd been some silences between them as darkness closed in, but those times felt easy and natural; neither of them had scrambled to fill the quiet with chatter. It had been a good conversation. It was close to nine o'clock when Ben checked his watch.

"I've really enjoyed this, Amy," he said. "But I've got to get home. My dad's due for a checkup, and his appointment's early. It's a five-hour drive, so . . ."

"Please give him my best, Ben. Tell him any friend of Zack's is a friend of mine."

"I'll do that."

They walked through the garage to the driveway and stood next to Ben's truck. "I know I'm sounding like a broken record, but thanks so much for Bobby. I'm still overwhelmed by your kindness."

"No need to be overwhelmed. The only thanks I need is for you and Bobby to become as close to one another as my old Zack was with me—and my new Zack will be."

The words touched Amy. Ben's delivery of them was far from dramatic, but it was clear that he meant what he said.

They faced one another, standing a foot apart next to Ben's truck, before he finally opened the door. Amy backed up a couple of steps, and Bobby moved back with her. She watched the red glow of the truck's taillights until they disappeared.

Amy had just sat down on her couch when her telephone rang. She hurried to the kitchen.

"Hi, Amy," Jake said. "Enjoying the new pup?"

"Wow." Amy laughed. "News travels fast out here."

"It sure does. I saw Ben in town today, and he told me what he'd done. I'm looking forward to meeting my new neighbor. Has he settled in yet? Sometimes that takes a few days, you know."

"Bobby—that's what I named him—seemed like he was at home the minute he got here. It's amazing, really. He's right here at my feet as if we've been together forever. He's a wonderful puppy. You'll love him."

"I'm sure I will. I'm sorry I wasn't able to stop by before today, but I've been all over the place for the last few days. I have a rodeo coming up, and I'm getting ready for that." He laughed. "You'd think after all these years I'd have all the details and all the minutia figured out—but I haven't. Every rodeo, I run around like I've never done any of it before."

"I saw your big trucks come in last night," Amy said. "How come you don't keep them at your ranch? It seems like it'd save you some time."

PAIGE LEE ELLISTON

"Wouldn't make sense to do it that way," Jake said. "I've got some acreage where I graze my bucking horses and where I keep the four bulls I own. I keep the trucks there, and all I need to do is load the horses—or the bulls, or both—and go on down the road to the rodeo. This time I brought the horses here to have Doc Pulver go over them before next weekend."

"You'll go for the weekend, then?"

"Yeah. I'll leave early Friday morning and get there in time for the evening show. Then there are two shows on Saturday and two on Sunday. It's a good rodeo—lots of talented cowboys."

"It must be exciting."

"It sure can be. I enjoy every minute of it, but the food . . . well, hot dogs and orange drink get old in a big hurry."

"I'm sure they do." Amy laughed. "Why not bring food with you?"

"No time to prepare it. I'm busy from the moment I hit the rodeo arena until the time I drive away a couple days later. Once I took stock to the Calgary Stampede in Canada, and I was there for eight solid days of nonstop rodeo. I felt like I needed a year in a rest home when I finished up."

"Didn't you have any help? Do you go alone?" Amy asked.

"Most of the time. It's pretty much a one-man operation, once the animals are unloaded. Sometimes Wes or one or more of my cowhands rides along with me, depending on the size of the rodeo. Actually, I kinda like getting away from the ranch once in a while."

131

Amy had run out of rodeo commentary. "Change every so often is good," she said, immediately feeling foolish at the blandness of what she'd said.

"Yeah. It is." He paused for a moment. "Uh, I was thinking, Amy . . . why don't you drive down to Porterville next Saturday and watch the rodeo with me? I can get you right up in the announcer's booth, where you won't miss a thing. Like I said, I'll be pretty busy, but I won't ignore you. And," he added, and she could hear the smile in his voice, "I'll even buy you a hot dog and an orange drink."

"Wow." Amy chuckled. "That sounds good, Jake. How far is Porterville?"

"It's not far. It's an easy drive. The town itself makes Coldwater look like Chicago, but they put on a heck of a rodeo every year."

"I wonder if I could . . ."

Jake anticipated her question. "If you keep Bobby on a leash, sure—bring him along. He'll be fine."

"That settles it, then. I'd love to come to your rodeo, Jake. I've never actually seen one. I've watched a couple of guys riding bucking broncos on TV sports shows, but that's about the extent of my experience."

"You'll like it," Jake assured her. "It's a good, clean, honest sport—no steroids or fancy million-dollar contracts or player lockouts. I'd bet you'll come away after Porterville a rodeo fan."

"Could be. Anyway, I'm looking forward to it."

"Good. I'll bring a pass and parking sticker when I come to see your pup later on in the week, OK?"

"That'll be fine. Thanks for calling and thanks for the invitation. I'll see you during the week."

Amy hung up the telephone and walked back to the couch. She turned off the lamp before she sat down—the light from the kitchen provided enough illumination for sitting and thinking. Bobby watched her for a minute, determined that she wasn't going to move right away, and stretched out on the rug.

Isn't this something? I have two great guys who appear to be interested in me. It's funny—I never did date more than one person at a time, even in high school. Now . . . But how do I know what Ben or Jake think about me—if they think about me at all. Maybe Ben is exactly what he seems to be: a kindhearted collie lover who saw a woman who didn't have a dog in her life and took things from there. Maybe, other than when he stops by to see Bobby on occasion, I'll never see him again. She shook her head. *I doubt that very much. I think we both felt a little something as we visited out in the backyard.*

Bobby was standing now, and he placed a tentative fore-paw on the couch and began to heft his body onto the cushion. "No," Amy said. The dog looked at her in the dusky light for a moment and then began to push himself up with his rear feet. "Bobby, no!" Amy said, louder and more sharply this time. The dog sighed audibly, backed away from the couch a bit, and settled himself on the carpet.

I can admit, at least to myself, that I'm attracted to Jake Winter. I have been since day one, I guess. And he's certainly shown interest in me. I'm sure it's more than the guy being a good neighbor, and I'm glad that's true. But with Mallory and her craziness, the things she said, what she seems to believe . . . But that's her problem, not mine, and there's nothing I can do about what she thinks or feels. Amy smiled to herself. *The rodeo next weekend will be fun. Maybe after a full day with Jake, I'll have a better feel for . . . what? What could happen between us?*

She stood and yawned. Images of both Jake and Ben flickered in her mind. *Not a bad problem to have,* she thought. Bobby and Nutsy followed her up the stairs to her room like creatures following Noah onto the ark.

6

Amy set her first cup of morning coffee on the counter and rotated the dial on her little transistor radio. Reception wasn't good, except for the Coldwater station. She tried that one for a few moments, gritting her teeth at the vivacious, smiley-voiced, morning host's babbling. She switched to a larger station for music, but the static was louder than the guitars. She snapped off the set and looked down at Bobby. His bowl was already empty. He'd hit his kibble like a starving wolf. Just now he was licking at the two little welts across his nose inflicted by Nutsy when he'd decided to try some of the kitten's food. Amy crouched in front of the dog.

"You'll get no sympathy from me, Bobby," she chided him. "I told you no, didn't I? Nutsy's food is as important to him as yours is to you." She grinned at her own silliness as the collie lapped at her face. Amy knew that when mature, Bobby would recognize or understand perhaps a couple dozen words, and that, except for the tone of voice used, talking to a dog made as much sense as talking to a cactus. Still, it was fun, and the pup already seemed to know his name and a couple of other words.

"Outdoors," she said. "Want to go outdoors, Bobby?"

The pup yelped excitedly, rushing toward the kitchen door to the outside. Nutsy finished his meal, watched the woman and the dog for a moment, and strode off to the living room for his morning nap.

Amy held the door open, and Bobby charged out and ran in a long half circle across the still dew-damp grass, galloping flat out for no other reason than that it felt good. He skidded to a stop in front of Amy and dropped his rawhide knot at her feet. She hadn't seen him snap it up from the ground on his run, but obviously he had. He stood, tail swinging, waiting for the throw. She was a little slow for Bobby's taste, and he barked at her to hurry her up.

As Amy cocked her arm to pitch the toy, she heard the thump of hoofbeats. She hurled the lump of rawhide and walked around the corner of her garage toward the sound.

It was easy to tell the rider was Mallory Powers by the luxurious blonde hair that trailed behind her in the breeze she and her horse were creating. She sat on the tall bay with the unconscious grace of a lifelong rider. It was almost as if the horse's moves—the gentle arcs and the quicker twists and turns—were choreographed for the event. Amy watched, enchanted by the woman's skill and her communion with the animal she rode and controlled.

Bobby stopped, and his toy dropped to the ground in front of him. He stood gaping, one forepaw raised an inch above the ground and his eyes focused on the huge animal running in the pasture beyond the fence. The breeze brought him the strange scent of this beast, and it was brand new to the puppy. As Mallory eased her mount through a fast figure eight, Bobby broke from his stance and raced toward the fence, driven by both instinct and curiosity. In his small mind, the creature was running from him, and his atavistic response was that of any dog: give chase. Amy yelled to the dog, but he, for the first time, ignored her call. He galloped toward the fence.

The fence was a three-rail post and rail with an electric line between the ground and the first rail and between the top of the first rail and the bottom of the second one. Bobby sailed over the lower electric wire cleanly and hustled toward the horse and rider. The bay went wide-eyed as the yapping dog approached.

Bobby charged directly at the horse, and the bay lost balance, skidded to the side, and lurched awkwardly off balance. Mallory handled the reins perfectly, shifting her weight to go with the momentum of the horse rather than against it, and held her seat as her mount caught himself before going down. He bucked a couple of times—crow hops, really—and attempted to run from the dog, but Mallory was able to rein him in.

Amy was sure that horse and rider were going to crash. She stood at the fence and called frantically for Bobby. Mallory's eyes pinned her in the same way a butterfly is pinned to a display board. Then she swung the bay to face the still-excited, still-barking dog, trying to show the horse there was nothing to be frightened of—no real danger to him.

Amy clambered up and over the fence, ignoring the sharp

137

jolt of an electrical shock when her leg brushed a wire, and ran toward the confrontation. She grabbed Bobby from the rear and lifted the squirming puppy to her chest. Her "Stop!" was almost a shriek, and it got Bobby's attention. He stopped his squirming and started panting from the excitement. Mallory walked her horse to within a few feet of Amy and Bobby and reined in, her face a mask of anger.

"That mutt almost cost a ten thousand dollar horse to have a wreck! He could have snapped a leg bone easily—making him as useless as your dog is. Don't you know enough to keep him chained up if he chases stock?"

"I'm sorry, Mallory," Amy said, her voice quivering. "I didn't know he'd—I didn't . . ."

"One of Jake's boys sees that dog out here running the mares, and he'll put a bullet in him, no questions asked—and I wouldn't blame him."

"I really didn't know that Bobby would—"

"Seems like there's a lot of stuff you don't know about living in the country," Mallory snarled. "Maybe you should've stayed in the city, where you belong."

Amy stripped the belt from her jeans with one hand and held the dog with the other. Then she put the belt through his collar and back through its own buckle, fashioning a makeshift leash. She looked back to Mallory. "I said I was sorry for all this," she said, her voice no longer trembling. "I can understand your being upset. I won't let it happen again." She paused for a moment. "But I'll tell you what: I don't need or want your opinion on what I do or where or how I live. You've been bitter toward me since the day we met. That's up to you—that's something I can't control. But I'm sick of it, and I won't listen to any more of it."

"You're not sick of my man, though, are you?"

Amy swallowed the hot reply that was a millisecond away from escaping her. Bobby, frightened by the tones in the voices he was hearing, by the tension in the air, tucked his face against Amy's shoulder. "I'm not going to dignify that with an answer," she said, voice level. "I meant what I said a moment ago, though. You don't like me, that's up to you. But I'm not going to put up with your craziness any longer."

"Is that a threat?" Mal asked. "Because if it is . . . ."

"Take it any way you want," Amy snapped. "Just keep out of my life."

Mallory wheeled the horse, spattering Amy with small clumps of sod and grass, and galloped away without another word, leaving a residue of rage—and perhaps even hatred—in her wake.

Amy led Bobby to the pasture fence, hefted him over it, and then climbed over herself, this time avoiding the electrical wires. The pup, tail between his legs, cringed in front of Amy as if she were going to hit him. "You know you were a bad boy, don't you?" she said gently. She turned Bobby to face where Mal was loping her horse in a wide circle. "No," Amy said sternly. "No." *He's a bright dog*, she thought. *If I repeat this often enough, he'll figure out that he needs to keep away from the horses.* She shuddered slightly with another thought. *If I wasn't here with Bobby, I have no idea what would have happened to him.*

139

It was two nights later, just at dusk when the day was beginning to cool, when Jake turned into Amy's driveway. Amy and Bobby, in the midst of a game of fetch with the beloved and now bedraggled rawhide knot, heard the truck and came to the front of the house from where they'd been playing in the back. As Jake got out of his truck, Bobby stepped in front of Amy protectively, watching this new person carefully. He didn't bark or growl, but his stance indicated that he was on guard, that he realized his job in life was to protect Amy. Jake was impressed, and so was Amy.

"That little guy knows his job already, doesn't he?" Jake said. "He's a beautiful collie, Amy. From the length of those legs and the breadth of his chest, it looks like he's going to be as big as his daddy. And if he's the dog Danny's Sunday is, you couldn't have a better companion. I'm real happy for you." He crouched down and extended his right hand. "C'mon, Bobby. How about saying hello?"

Amy touched the pup's hip lightly. "Go on, Bobby," she urged him. "Jake's a friend. Go look him over." Within a few moments after sniffing the offered hand and accepting some soft words and some stroking, Bobby was dancing between his new friend and Amy, basking in the affection of both of them as they walked around the garage to the backyard.

Even in the fading light Amy could see that Jake's eyes were a bit bloodshot and that there was a tension in his face she hadn't seen before. "You look tired, Jake," she said. "Long day?"

"Too long," Jake admitted. "I had to go over to Porterville early to check out the new chutes they put in and make sure I'd have enough room in back of the gates for my stock pens." He sighed. "Maybe if the cowboys were riding prairie dogs, there'd have been enough room. Some self-styled rodeo architect had figured everything just about as wrong as it could possibly be." He shook his head wearily. "So, what should have been a quick inspection kept me there for five hours. Then we ran out of fencing—the pipes for the pens—and couldn't locate . . . ahhh, nuts. You don't need to hear all this." He managed to put a grin on his face, but it was strained. "Anyway, I'm glad the day is finally over. I wanted to meet Bobby tonight, because I'll be back at the Porterville fairgrounds again tomorrow and maybe the next day."

"I'm glad you came, Jake." She touched his shoulder. "The good thing about horrid days is that they end. How about collapsing into the lawn chair while I get us some iced tea. Or would you rather have coffee?"

"Tea would be good. I'm about coffee-ed out today. Thanks."

"You look like you could use something to eat," Amy said. "I don't have much of anything on hand, but I picked up some cold cuts and a quart of potato salad from the market today. What do you say?"

This time the smile was real. "Amy, I'd give you your weight in uncut diamonds for a sandwich, and I love potato salad."

Amy laughed. "The diamonds aren't necessary—but greatly appreciated, anyway. Give me a couple minutes." As she walked to the house, Jake extended his legs in front of him, crossed his boots at the ankle, and relaxed for what was the first time in several hours.

The drink, sandwich, and two helpings of potato salad reinvigorated Jake. "That was great, Amy. Just what I needed," he said, setting his plate and glass on the picnic table.

Amy moved her lawn chair a bit closer to Jake. They watched Bobby chasing insects, his milk teeth clacking together as he attacked. "Mighty hunter," Jake observed. "If I slammed my jaws together like that, I'd need thousands of dollars worth of orthodontia."

They talked comfortably as they watched the sun begin to set. Amy took Jake's dishes inside, and when she returned she saw he'd moved the two chairs close together. She smiled and sat without commenting. Jake reached over and touched her hand.

"I heard you had a run-in with Mallory."

"Yeah. I've had Bobby along the fence several times today near your mares, telling him no. He's catching on. There won't be any more horse chasing."

"I don't know how much damage he could really do unless he ran a panicked horse through a fence or something," Jake said. "But it's good he's learning. He's going to be seeing horses for a long time." He hesitated for a moment. "But that's not the point. Mallory overreacted. There was no reason for that."

"Well, she was angry. But I agree, she overreacted. There was no reason for some of the things she said to me. I . . . I simply don't understand her."

"I don't know that I do, either." The hand that had touched

Amy's now came to it again, this time holding it. Their fingers intertwined naturally, as if they'd held hands many times before.

"She's hard to figure out at times," Jake went on. "She has a lot to offer—she's pretty and bright and can be as sweet as a kitten at times. A heck of a trainer too. I really . . . well . . . anyway, I'm sorry about what happened. I'll talk to her about it."

"That's not necessary. Let's let the whole thing go, OK? It's not worth causing more trouble over."

Fireflies had begun to flash their signals to one another by the time Jake released Amy's hand. "I'd better get home," he said. "I still have a couple calls to make. I think I have a vet lined up for the rodeo, but I need to confirm. I waited too long on that, assuming I had Danny again this year." They stood and walked to the front of the house. Bobby, tired from his bug hunt, walked behind the couple.

They stood at Jake's truck. For a heartbeat, Amy was certain Jake was going to lean forward and kiss her. He seemed to be thinking the same thing, but he didn't act on it. Still, Amy knew that something had happened tonight, something that brought them closer together, that brought them beyond strictly neighborly feelings.

"Thanks again for the feed, Amy."

"Any time at all."

"Well, then," Jake said. He climbed into his truck. He was suddenly grinning like a ten-year-old at a birthday party. "This was good." He started his engine and backed down the driveway.

143

"It *was* good," Amy said to the darkness.

The coffee in Amy's Mr. Coffee had been on the burner too long for her taste; she dumped it in the sink and prepared another half pot. When it had completed its cycle she poured a cup and returned to her spot at the kitchen table. Bobby and Nutsy sat side by side on the floor and stared up at her, hoping for a bit of table scrap even though she wasn't eating anything.

Amy shifted uncomfortably in her chair, straightened her back, and prepared to type. "Let's get to it, girl," she said aloud. Her voice must have conveyed some tension. Bobby started, his eyes on her face. Nutsy industriously licked his paw, paying no attention to the words that had bothered the dog. Amy reached down and rubbed Bobby's neck until his tail wagged. "I wasn't talking to you," she assured him.

She pecked out a scene. It wasn't the most vivid episode she'd ever written, but it wasn't terrible, either. The lines of dialogue that wound through the description and action sounded logical and natural as she read them aloud. *Better than nothing*, she thought. *If I can keep it moving . . .*

The ringing of the telephone startled her. She took a deep breath before she walked to the telephone. "Amy Hawkins."

"Hey, Amy. It's Ben. I thought I'd call and check on how Bobby is getting on."

Amy's face broke into a smile. "Hi, Ben. He's doing just great. He's learning new stuff every day." She imitated a drumroll. "And he hasn't made a single mistake in the house.

He goes to the door and whines or scratches at it when he needs to go out. What a dog, no?"

"That's great. Some of them are like that—my first Zack was. This Zack is much the same way, but I have to admit I've discovered a couple of damp spots behind the couch. They were probably my fault, though. I might have left him alone too long when I was held up on a job or doing an estimate. A pup can only hang on so long."

"I've been pretty scrupulous about taking Bobby out frequently. Actually, it's a good break for both of us. It does me good to get up from my laptop and breathe some fresh air."

"I bet. How's the book coming?"

"Slow but . . . semi-sure, I guess."

"You've never told me what it's about. I'd really like to know."There was obvious interest in Ben's voice—he wasn't asking only to keep the conversation rolling until he could get to the real reason he'd called.

"Well, I need to give you a preface first. My roommate in college was from Oklahoma, and she had a couple of diaries her great-grandmother had kept during the years of the Great Depression . . ." She went on synopsizing the plot, explaining the characters, trying to sketch the conflict and drama inherent in the story. When she was finished she drew a breath. "Whew! I'm sure I've told you more than you wanted to know."

"Not at all. It sounds fascinating—it really does. Ya know, my dad lived through the tail end of the depression here in Montana. You might want to talk to him sometime. He has lots of stories he loves to tell about those times."

"I'd like to do that."

"And he'd love the opportunity. He has a great story about when he used to ride an old plow horse to grammar school each day."

As Ben went on about his father's tale, Amy couldn't help but compare the conversation she was having with Ben with Jake's stilted, self-conscious first telephone call. She grinned at the memory: *"I don't much like talking on the telephone."*

"Amy?"

"I'm here, Ben. Sorry."

"Anyway, the reason I called is because I was wondering if you'd like to grab something to eat at the café tonight and then come over to my place so I can show off a sideboard I'm making for a customer. I've just started the finishing, but the structure is complete. I'm really proud of this one, and I'd like you to see it."

"Oh, Ben—I'd love to, but I really can't tonight. I'm sorry. Can we do it another night?"

The silence was a little longer than Amy thought it should have been. "Sure, we can do it another night. I'll call again, and we can set it up, OK?"

The conversation fizzled to a tepid conclusion. *You absolute moron!* Amy badgered herself the very second she hung up. *The novel would have kept for another few hours. What in the world were you thinking? A nice guy like Ben—the guy who brought Bobby into my life—and I can't spend a few hours with him?*

And it's not only gratitude for Bobby, she chided herself. *I genuinely like Ben. Being with him the other night was something special.*

Amy walked away from the telephone and took her place at her computer. She'd clicked it off when she answered the telephone; now she turned it back on. *Some kind of Freudian thing? I didn't think I'd come back to work after my call?* She watched the screen fill with figures and icons and listened to the mechanical mumblings of the boot-up process. She accessed her book's next page on the screen and poised her hands over the keyboard, in a somewhat sloppy approximation of the basic position demanded by typing teachers. And then . . .

And then, nothing.

For this I turned down a date with Ben Callan?

She jammed her chair back and strode into the living room, her gait as stiff as it would be if she were marching in a parade. Amy Hawkins didn't frequently get mad at herself, but she was just that now. Her thoughts attacked her. *I know exactly what the people around here would tell me to do: "Quit your whining and get a job, lady." If writing books doesn't work, you need to do something else. Being a starving writer is poignant and dramatic in novels—but in the real world it's simply stupid, or lazy, or both.*

Amy felt eyes on her as she stood glaring out the picture window, and she turned to face into the room. Bobby and Nutsy were sitting side by side and staring at her. Neither animal moved. Amy looked into their eyes and felt her anger begin to melt. It was perfectly still in the living room—in the entire house—as if the animals' concentration on her had washed away all sounds.

The staring contest seemed to go on for a very long time. Amy read the love in the eyes of her animals. Her shoulders relaxed slightly, and she unclenched her hands. Then, as if on some cue that Amy wasn't aware of, Nutsy broke eye contact and began licking a forepaw. Bobby too looked away, nodded his head as if agreeing to something, and burped loudly. Amy collapsed to her knees in laughter, pulling the pup and the cat close to her, hugging them until they squirmed to get loose. Then she fell backward onto the carpet, stretched out her legs, and gazed up at the ceiling. *I'll do what I need to do. If I have to find a job of some kind to keep things together here, that's what I'll do. I'm not broke yet—I still have some money, I still have some time to write before the bottom drops out. And one way or another—soon or in the future—I'll finish* The Longest Years, *and I'll be proud of it.*

Bobby whined at the back door, and Amy realized she was hearing him for the second or third time in the past few minutes. She clambered to her feet and hurried to the door. Bobby opened it the last few inches with his body as he hustled by her and squatted almost immediately within a few feet of the house. Relieved, the dog found his rawhide knot and brought it back to Amy. She was about to throw it when she heard hoofbeats in the pasture. The thudding stopped Bobby too. He forgot about the game of fetch and swung his head toward Jake's pasture. "Bobby," Amy said, her voice steady. "No." The pup held his pose for a long moment, still gazing toward the pasture. Then, he turned to Amy and waited for her throw.

"Good boy," Amy said. "Goooood boy, Bobby." They walked around the edge of her garage; Bobby kept perfect pace with her strides.

Wes Newton was on his gray horse, urging one of the mares to leave the others and head for the steel building. The mare was reluctant, but Wes's horse performed like a dog herding sheep, turning the mare, driving her toward the building. Wes saw Amy and waved; he raised the loop of lariat he carried to greet her. He called something to another cowhand sitting on his horse near the back fence, and the cowboy spurred his horse, formed a loop from his lariat, and tossed it over the mare's head, making the entire process look as easy as smiling at a friend. Wes rode to the fence and reined up close to it, waiting for Amy to walk over.

He eyed Bobby. "Looks like the pup learned his lesson, Ms. Amy. I watched you get after him after he ran Mal's horse. I gotta say this—you handled your dog just right. Whaling on a good dog doesn't accomplish a thing, but your no worked jus' fine."

"Bobby's a quick learner," Amy said. "I didn't see you out in the pasture when all that happened. I guess I wasn't seeing much but Mallory's horse and my dog."

"I was out back there, hooking up the bush hog to the tractor. I seen an' heard a good part of it."

"You heard what Mallory said about Jake, then?"

Wes nodded. "'Bout him being her man and all that? Yeah, I heard it." He shifted in his saddle and rested the hand holding the reins atop the saddle horn. "I wouldn't pay much attention to anything she says."

"She certainly lit into Bobby and me. I know my dog was in the wrong and that Jake's horses are expensive, but—"

"Wasn't no reason for all the raggin' on you," Wes interrupted. "That pup of yours maybe never before saw a horse in motion. That's why he had to chase it. I've seen you playing with him when the mares was out grazing, and the pup didn't pay them any mind."

"Well, there's no sense in my worrying about it now," Amy said.

Wes nodded. After a moment, he said, "I hear you're goin' to the rodeo Saturday."

"Yep." Amy smiled. "I'm looking forward to it. It's my first time, except for what little I've seen on TV."

"It's a whole other thing when you see it live, right in front of you. I wish I could go along, but Jake's got me here, kinda running things while he's gone."

Amy was about to respond when the cowhand who'd roped the mare whistled shrilly and called for Wes.

"Speakin' of which," Wes said, "looks like Wade's havin' some trouble getting that ol' gal inside." He tipped his hat to Amy, wheeled his horse, and set out at a fast lope. Bobby whined deep in his throat as he watched the horse race away, but he didn't move from his place next to Amy.

Together they walked to Amy's front door. Instead of going in immediately, Amy sat on the top step of her porch, Bobby next to her. The silence was broken by the faint sound of feminine laughter coming from the direction of Jake's house. It irritated her, and she felt foolish that it did. When she heard the laughter the second time, she took her dog and went inside, slamming the door behind her.

Saturday morning Amy was up and showered by 6:00 a.m. As she fed the animals and started her coffee, she let her mind take her where it would. She remembered the velvet evening with the embers of the fire in the grill fading to a dim red, and the plates and empty cups on the picnic table marking their meal. It was the end of a fine evening—and perhaps the beginning of something else. And today she'd spend the entire day with Jake.

Bobby picked up on Amy's excitement as she moved about the kitchen, humming happily, packing her Igloo cooler with the thermos of iced tea, half an apple pie, a pint of French vanilla ice cream, and two huge roast beef sandwiches on oversized Coldwater bakery rolls. In a separate bag Amy carried two servings of Bobby's kibble, his rawhide toy, a handful of paper napkins, and two small bags of potato chips. She glanced around the kitchen to make sure she hadn't forgotten anything, clicked Bobby's new leash to his freshly purchased collar, and led him through the door to the garage. He hopped into the Jeep as soon as Amy opened the door, and situated himself on the passenger seat, as anxious to get rolling as Amy was.

A good day, Amy thought as she backed out of the garage. *This will be a good day.*

The weather couldn't have been much better. The sun

151

smiled down from a deep azure sky, with only snippets of pure white clouds appearing toward the western horizon. It was cooler than average for late July in Montana—seventy-eight degrees—which made it ideal for rodeo.

The map Amy downloaded from her laptop wasn't necessary since the run to Porterville was a one-highway trip. She rolled through Coldwater, making the one traffic light, and set her cruise control at sixty-eight when she hit the open highway. She marveled at the beauty of the prairie around her and at the fact that she'd so rapidly and completely left civilization behind. She was alone on the road without another vehicle visible either in front of or behind her Jeep. Rather than click on the air-conditioning, Amy lowered her window and the one next to Bobby a few inches and let the fresh air circulate through the vehicle. Bobby stuck his snout out through the opening, and the breeze pushed his tongue to the side like the trailing necktie of a hurrying businessman.

The "Porterville—12 Miles" sign appeared on Amy's right side. It, like many of the state and local signs she'd seen in rural Montana, allowed light to peep through a series of punctures in the metal—indications that hunters had used the signs to sight in their high-powered rifles. Amy grinned. Sure, it was damage to state property. But, in a perverse way, the bullet holes were a manifestation of the Old West spirit and attitude of her adopted slice of America. When she saw a hand-lettered sign in front of a farmhouse, saying, "Old Records and Books for Sale," her grin expanded to a full smile at the happy realization that in the months she'd lived in Coldwater she hadn't seen the word *old* spelled *olde* a single time.

The rodeo posters, bright and colorful, tacked to power poles and to the posts that supported the mailboxes of the occasional farm or ranch, began to appear about ten miles outside Porterville. Amy passed a pair of teens on horseback—a boy and a girl—both dressed in what appeared to be their best Western clothing. *Rodeo fans*, she thought. She gave them plenty of room as she pulled by.

The fairground was easy enough to find—Amy followed the signs and arrows. It consisted of several acres of unpaved parking lot surrounding a long rectangle of bleacher-type seating. Although the first show of the day wasn't scheduled until 2:00 p.m., a haze of dust hung over the parking area, and pale blue smoke rose from the grills of the concession stands. Bobby, now standing on the passenger seat with his forepaws braced on the window ledge, couldn't seem to move his head rapidly enough to take in the new sights or sniff the air greedily enough to absorb the myriad scents. "I know, Bobby," Amy said to the collie. "It's all brand new to me too."

There didn't seem to be any protocol to parking. Pickup trucks, cars, and vans were arranged in ragged rows, with a cluster of larger trucks and horse trailers in a roped-off section at one end of the rectangle of seating. Amy immediately noticed that one of Jake's large stock trucks was backed up to an open gate. Men—all of whom were dressed in jeans and boots and wore cowboy hats—meandered about inside the roped-in area. Several of them carried clipboards. A couple of them tossed loops at upended buckets. One intense young cowboy sat on a bale of hay as if it were a horse and swept his legs back and forth as if spurring a bronc.

Amy parked next to a pickup with a decal reading "Bull Riding—America's #1 Sport," hooked Bobby's leash to his collar, and stepped out of her Jeep into the world of Montana rodeo. She walked beyond the parking area to let Bobby relieve himself and then headed back to the main entrance to the arena—the area where the concessions and booths were set up. The scent of coffee had reached her, and the fact that almost everyone she saw carried a steaming Styrofoam cup sent her to a Porterville Chamber of Commerce booth advertising "The Best Coffee in the World." Heads turned as Amy and Bobby walked by. Women smiled at her, and men nodded and grinned. One old gent in a wheelchair winked at her and said, "Handsome dog you got there."

Amy bought a cup of coffee—*Twenty-five cents? It would have been two-fifty at a fair or festival in New York*—and wandered toward the bleacher seating inside the rectangle. A small tractor was dragging the dirt of the arena floor and putting a cloud of grit into the air behind it as it chugged along. The numbered chutes the riders and animals would emerge from comprised the end of the arena farthest from Amy. Above the chutes was the announcer's booth, a square structure with an open, glassless, picture-window-type view of the arena. Country-western music played through the scratchy, static-ridden public address system. Amy watched the men around the booth, hoping to see Jake. It didn't really surprise her that she didn't find him gabbing and laughing with the cowboys and the announcer's staff. He'd told her he had to be in a dozen places all at the same time until a show got rolling and he had some time to watch the action. She recalled the excitement in Jake's voice as he described the events to her. *He loves this stuff*, she'd thought then. *He really and truly loves it. It's not a way to make a living with his animals—it's a major part of his life.*

Both Amy and Bobby were fascinated by the sights, sounds, and smells around them. There was a freshness, a scent of newly painted wood and good strong coffee, of prairie breeze and burning charcoal and mesquite, of polished leather and arena dust, that helped make the experience a captivating one.

Wade, a cowhand employee of Jake's that Amy had seen around several times, caught her eye from the booth and waved to her. She led Bobby over to the man and smiled at the crispness of the Western shirt he wore and the actual crease in his jeans.

"You're looking good, Wade," she said.

The cowhand blushed as he crouched to stroke Bobby. "You aren't looking half bad yourself," he said. "I didn't know you were a rodeo fan."

"Well," she admitted, "this is my first one. Jake invited me to watch from the announcer's booth with him, so I guess we'll have the best seats in the house." She watched a young guy in huge, raggedy pants, a falling-apart shirt, and a massive cowboy hat walk away from the group at the booth. "I get a kick out of the clowns. They must go over great with the kids who—"

155

"Uh . . . Amy?" Wade interrupted.

"What?"

"Those boys—don't call them clowns around rodeo people," he said, his eyes holding hers. "They're called bull-fighters, and they have the most dangerous job in rodeo. All of us—fans and contractors and especially the guys who ride—have nothin' but respect for the bullfighters."

"I didn't know," Amy said. "Thanks for setting me straight."

They stood together for a moment, surrounded by the movement and the color. "Have you seen Jake?" Amy asked. "I saw his truck over behind the chutes, but I haven't seen him yet."

Wade pointed to the rear of the arena. "He's probably lookin' after the stock. They got him set up off behind where the trucks and the competitors parking is—kinda beyond where you saw Jake's stock van." Then, Wade pointed directly across the arena. "They got him a travel trailer to stay in—a big Airstream—parked over there, all hooked up with electric and water. If he isn't with the stock or in the booth, he's probably at the trailer."

"I'm sure I'll find him sooner or later." Amy smiled. "Thanks, Wade. See you later. I want to explore some more."

Wade tipped his Stetson and returned her smile. "You enjoy your first rodeo, now," he said.

Amy nodded. "I'm sure I will." It had been a grand day so far, and the actual rodeo didn't even start for several hours.

More vehicles—mostly pickup trucks—were filling the spaces in the parking lot. People greeted friends, and laughter and the squeals of young children seemed to drown out the unrequited-love song rasping out of the pole-mounted speakers. Bobby paced at Amy's side, every so often moving closer and licking the hand that held his leash. Once, a handsome chocolate Lab glared at Bobby as the pup yipped a greeting. Amy grinned as the Lab's throaty growl sent Bobby tight against her legs.

She stopped at a hot dog stand and asked for a bowl of water for Bobby, which was immediately handed over with a couple of ice cubes floating in it. Again, Amy marveled at the grace and attitude of the people she'd come across in Montana.

Bobby drinking a good part of a quart of cold water made it necessary to find a place for him to get rid of some of it. Amy walked well beyond the parking lot to a stand of scruffy desert pines that afforded a small splash of shade. She allowed her pup to select a spot, and then she sat in the grass with her back against the trunk of a pine. The sounds of the fairgrounds reached her, but everything was softened by the two hundred yards between the rodeo and the stand of trees. She rested in the shade, idly stroking Bobby's back as he stretched out next to her.

After ten minutes or so Amy stood and brushed the grass from her jeans. Bobby stood too, looking up at her, tail moving from side to side slowly, questioningly. "Back to the rodeo," she said. "Let's see if we can find the guy who asked us here today." She checked her watch; it was going on noon. The parking area, she noticed as she walked back, was filled to its capacity, and new arrivals were stashing their trucks and cars in the pitted, overgrown acres beyond the ground that had been cleared. Others—those with four-wheel drive—braved a wet couple of acres that would trap and hold normal vehicles.

Jake's bucking horses were grazing in a pipe enclosure much like the one Amy had seen in Jake's indoor arena. Two bulls, their coats shiny brass, stood in a separate enclosure, looking as peaceful as a pair of sleepy kittens. Bobby eyed the bulls but kept pace with Amy, not hanging back for a longer look. Beyond the corrals Amy could see down the side of the arena to where, about at its midpoint, a travel trailer stood next to a power pole. The sun had begun bearing down, and Amy realized how thirsty she was. She envisioned the tall glass of iced tea—or ice water or anything cold and wet—she hoped would be waiting for her in the Airstream.

The pre-rodeo show had started inside the arena. As the final notes of the "Star Spangled Banner" floated across the prairie, the jubilant thunder of the crowd's cheering followed. Whatever happened next in the arena brought laughter and then more cheering from the audience as Amy trudged toward the trailer.

The heat was beginning to get to her; she tugged a handkerchief from the pocket of her jeans and wiped her forehead. Her mouth and throat felt like she'd eaten a sack of sand. She glanced at Bobby and saw that his tongue was limp, dry, coated with dust; he was as thirsty as she was. She quickened her pace. Bobby, at first reluctant, felt the urgency and hurried along with her.

The trailer was situated so that the hookup was toward Amy and the entrance to it faced the fairgrounds arena. It was larger than most of the trailers Amy had seen on the road. The chrome fittings of the unit were shiny and reflected the sunlight like the finish of a polished car. The sound of Jake's laughter—faint but unmistakable to Amy—reached her. She opened her mouth, ready to call out to him—and then she stopped walking so quickly that Bobby hit the end of his leash and was yanked off his front feet for a second.

Intertwined with Jake's masculine laughter, the voice of a woman—and the laughter of one—floated to Amy across the twenty or so yards that separated her from the trailer. The angle put the pull-down awning over the door in her view, and as she moved to the side, she was able to see the three metal steps that led to the ground.

On the steps Mallory stood with her arm loosely around Jake's waist, laughing again. There was a yellow bath towel draped around Mallory's neck, and even at the distance it was easy to see that her hair was wet—fresh from the shower. Mallory leaned into Jake, turned her head to him, got up on her toes, and kissed him on the cheek.

Amy watched as the couple descended the steps. There seemed to be a marital quality to the moment, a casual but intimate intensity. Jake, his back now to Amy, said something to Mallory that Amy couldn't hear. Mallory laughed again, and the tinkling sound struck Amy's heart like an arrow.

Jake and Mallory were unaware that they were being

159

observed. Amy scuttled to the side, putting the end of the Airstream between herself and the couple. After a moment she turned away, tugged at Bobby's leash, and began the walk back to her Jeep. The few seconds of what she'd seen replayed in her mind as vividly as a movie on a screen. She swallowed hard as she walked, trying to force down the painful lump of emotion that had risen in her throat. The parking lot and her Jeep seemed very far away, just as far away as what she'd been fantasizing about Jake Winter.

The announcer's voice, distorted by the inefficient PA system and the distance, welcomed everyone to the Porterville Rodeo and promised them they'd have a day to remember.

7

Amy pulled a page advertising car insurance from under her windshield wiper, crumpled it into a tight ball, and tossed it into her backseat after she unlocked the door of her Jeep. She took Bobby's bowl and a bottle of water from the cooler and poured the liquid into the bowl. Bobby lapped it up quickly. She opened another bottle for herself and drank deeply. After a moment she recapped the bottle, motioned Bobby to his spot on the passenger seat, and climbed in behind the wheel. A fine film of dust and grit had settled on Amy's windshield. She started her engine, turned on the wipers, and pressed the washer button. In a quick minute the windshield was clean, but there was still a shimmery texture to her vision. She wiped her eyes with the back of her hand angrily and shifted into first gear, spinning her tires as she pulled away from her parking spot and rocked across the field to the road.

Again, there was next to no traffic. Once Amy passed through Porterville, there was none at all. It was as if she was alone in the universe. *OK, I'm a fool. I admit it—just like I was a fool with Tom.* She wiped her sleeve across her eyes. *Maybe I'm not quite as smart as I thought I was about relationships since my disaster with Tom, but I saw something happening between Jake and me. Was I completely wrong about that? Is he a good enough actor to pull me into some sort of a triangle? Why would he do that? What's the benefit to him? Or, is he one of these "new millennium" guys who can't—or refuse to—commit to exclusivity, to love?*

Bobby whined in his sleep, and Amy scratched his side, keeping her eyes on the road.

The ride was uneventful. She wasn't quite sure whether the tears she wiped away every so often were from sadness or from anger, but after a while they no longer came.

Amy pulled into her driveway and tucked her Jeep into the garage, thumbing the button on the door control to close the overhead. She entered her home through the door into the kitchen, for once ignoring the cheerful scents and welcoming atmosphere, and walked woodenly into the living room, where she dropped onto the couch. Bobby stopped at his bowl with his leash dragging behind him. After cleaning up the scraps he'd left earlier that morning, he stretched out in front of Amy, ready for a nap.

The house was midday quiet. Amy hugged a pillow to her chest and rested her heels on the coffee table in front of her. She couldn't stop thinking about Jake and Mallory.

"I don't need this!" Amy said loudly enough and sharply enough to startle Bobby from a sound sleep. *Is this another phony romance, another Tom, that I'm becoming involved in here? Not this girl! I had enough pain and tears the last time around. This . . . this drugstore cowboy had me fooled.*

162

A hard little smile that wasn't really a smile appeared on Amy's face. *Good—it's better to be angry than to be hurt*, she told herself. *One Tom in my life was enough—much more than enough. I'm not going to let Jake Winter or any other man hurt me like that again.*

Too agitated to sit still now, Amy tossed her pillow aside and began pacing, her boot heels loud against the hardwood and quiet as she walked on carpeted areas. The sounds—the end of the heavy silence—seemed to help lift her mood slightly. Bobby, anticipating a game of some sort, followed a half step behind Amy. She was a stride beyond the wall telephone in the kitchen when it rang. Amy stopped, and Bobby banged his nose against the back of her knee. She turned, allowed the phone to ring twice more, and then answered. Even before she spoke she heard the crowd and the announcer's voice as loud as if the rodeo was being held in her living room.

"Amy Hawkins," she said. Her voice sounded tight and hostile, even to her own ears.

The audience racket at the other end of the line swelled, and the announcer shouted something unintelligible to Amy, something that ended, ". . . put a fine ride on that little pinto from Jake Winter's string."

"I shouldn't have called from the booth," Jake said. "I was worried that something had happened, an accident or something." He waited for a moment. "Amy? You there?"

"What is it you want, Jake? Why did you bother calling me?"

"I . . . I don't understand. Is something wrong? We had

plans to spend today together, right?" He said something else, but audience noise swallowed the words.

"This is ridiculous." Amy snorted. "I can't hear you. Come to think of it, I don't even want to hear you. Good-bye, Jake."

She banged the receiver into place as if the telephone was somehow the cause of the problem. Almost immediately, it began ringing again. Amy fumbled around on the side of the instrument's plastic casing, found the tiny ringer-mute switch, and clicked it forward, slicing a ring in half. Then, the telephone was quiet. "There," she said. She watched the phone for a moment and then went back into the living room and flopped down onto the couch. As she reached for the throw pillow, a thought stopped her in midmotion.

Suppose I'm wrong? Suppose the whole thing was completely innocent? She shook her head. *I know what I saw, what I heard. They laughed together; she had her arm around him. She kissed him, for goodness sake!*

But no matter what Amy had seen, she had a hard time believing that Jake would string her along, that he would pursue her and Mallory at the same time. *I'm not that poor a judge of character.*

She sighed. *Still, the truth is that even if everything seemed to be moving slowly, maybe in my mind it was going fast. Jake is entitled to his feelings. Maybe he should be my neighbor, my friend—and nothing more.*

Amy was glad when Bobby scratched at the back door a half hour later. She'd been staring at the wall of her living

164

room, playing an endless tape of Jake and Mallory in her mind. She opened the door and followed the collie into the backyard. It wasn't quite five o'clock, and the sun had not yet started on its downward swing. She breathed the hot air deeply and meandered after Bobby as he searched for precisely the right place.

Amy was surprised and curious when Bobby dropped his rawhide toy and snapped to attention, facing the front of the house, ears pricked. A half second later she heard hooves in her driveway and Wes's voice calling, "Miss Amy! Hey, Miss Amy!"

She walked around the garage to the front yard. A tall, rangy black horse stood in the driveway. Wes, on the porch steps, called to her again. "Miss Amy, you here?"

"I'm right here, Wes," she answered the old cowhand.

He turned and took off his Stetson. "Well," he said. His face showed concern and perhaps some confusion. "I wasn't sure you were OK. I was just checkin'."

"Why wouldn't I be OK?"

"Well . . . see, Jake called me not more'n a few minutes ago, all worried. He said you was supposed to be at Porterville, and when he called you, you sounded strange. He asked me to check and make sure you were all right. I tossed a saddle on a horse and hustled over."

Amy forced a smile. "As you can see, I'm fine, Wes. Thanks for coming, though. I appreciate your concern."

"Well," Wes repeated. After a long moment, he said, "I recall you told me you were going to the rodeo. Then, I seen you early this morning setting out with Bobby sitting next to you." He paused again. "Something happen to your car, Miss Amy?"

"No. I got there. Then I came home."

"But, then, why ain't you . . ."

Amy shook her head. "I don't want to go into it right now, Wes. I'm sorry."

Wes nodded. He put his hat back on. "Maybe there's something I can do for you?" he asked gently.

"No . . . no, thanks."

"OK, then," Wes said. "Should I tell Jake you were there at the rodeo?"

She shrugged and looked at the ground. "If you want to."

The old cowhand made eye contact with her. "I guess maybe you saw Mallory there in Porterville."

Amy made a dismissive motion with her hand, not quite trusting her voice.

"Miss Amy, you gotta understand—"

"Please, Wes, let's not talk about it now."

"OK," he said. "One other thing: Jake tol' me to tell you he'd be coming over here Sunday night soon's he gets back from Porterville. He wanted me to be real sure I told you that."

Amy sighed. "Thanks for delivering the message, Wes. I . . . I gotta get inside now. Good night."

Wes reached up with his right hand to tip the brim of his Stetson, but Amy's back was already to him as she headed for her front door at a fast walk. Amy watched through the picture window as the old man rode down the driveway toward the road, his shoulders slightly slumped and his back not quite as rifle-barrel straight as it usually was.

≈≈

Sunday dawned sunny, bright, and warm. Amy went through her morning ritual—shower, start coffee, go out with Bobby, feed Nutsy and Bobby, drink coffee—just as she did every morning. She'd slept poorly, and the bright sunlight began to generate a throbbing headache during the short time she was outside with her pup.

Ian's early service, as usual, was well attended. Amy sat toward the rear of the small church, nodding to those people she knew, offering a smile to those she didn't. Ian's sermon, which covered charity and unselfishness, was interesting and well presented. She found comfort in the church and the muted light streaming through the new stained glass window and in the words of Ian Lane. She promised herself she'd take a closer look at her charitable contributions. And, she decided, she could spend some time each week as a volunteer at the animal shelter or the hospital—whichever needed help the most. The images of Jake and Mallory hadn't faded from her mind, but the elapsed twenty-four hours offered some distance from the sharpness of the pain.

The fellowship hour following the service brought Amy and Julie together at the coffee table. Danny, Julie explained, had been called away at 4:30 that morning to attend at the birth of a foal and had gotten home at 8:00 and fallen into bed, exhausted. His visiting friend, also a veterinarian, had gone with him on the call. He, too, was still sleeping. "So, here I am, alone. How's your weekend been?" she asked Amy.

Amy stepped a little closer to her friend. "Horrendous. I'll tell you about it next time we get together."

"How about now? The men will be sleeping, and we can sit outside and talk."

Amy considered the offer and then declined. "Not today, Julie—but thanks. I've got to put the whole mess straight in my mind before I can talk about it and make any sense."

"Sounds serious," Julie observed. "You sure you don't want some company? I can come to your place if you like."

"Thanks, Julie, but no. Not today. I'll call you during the week, OK?"

"Sure," Julie agreed. "That'll be good. I'll look forward to your call."

Two other women joined them, and as the talk turned to church projects and then horses, Amy was able to slip away. She finished her coffee, tossed the Styrofoam cup in the trash basket, and headed to the parking lot. As she started her Jeep she mentally kicked herself for turning down Julie's invitation. *It'd be good to talk to Julie, to share what I'm feeling with a person I respect and trust and feel safe with. So, why didn't I do it?* Still arguing with herself, she started her engine and drove out of the lot and away from the church.

Halfway home, Amy slowed, foot hovering over the brake pedal, and waved to one of the girls from the bakery in town who was riding on the opposite shoulder of the road, her horse looking shiny and freshly shampooed. The teenager—Kristin, Amy recalled her name—recognized the Jeep and waved.

A dark cloud moved into Amy's mind as she resumed speed. *Could the reason that I didn't want to get together with Julie for a talk today be that I realize on some level that I've blown the entire situation with Jake Winter out of proportion? Was I assuming too much about us—wanting too much?*

Bobby, on a light staked chain in the early morning shade of the garage, yipped a greeting to Amy as she pulled into the driveway. Not only his tail but his entire hindquarters whipped from side to side with happiness. She went to the dog and unhooked the chain from his collar. Bobby danced at her feet and then dashed off to fetch his toy, which he brought back and offered to her as if it were a piece of fine jewelry.

"No time to play, Bobby," she told the collie. "I have things to do."

Things like what? Sitting in front of my laptop like a lump of clay, waiting to see if Jake will really show up here tonight? Yeah, I have important things to do, all right.

She took the proffered, saliva-dampened rawhide knot, leaned back, and hurled it as far as her best pitch would take it. Bobby streaked after it. The game continued until Bobby was tired and Amy's throwing arm was sore.

Just now, her home didn't radiate the sensation of welcome that Amy so enjoyed. It seemed impersonal—like a hotel room in a strange city—and was without the warmth that generally greeted her as she walked inside. Standing just inside the front door, she looked around her living room and into the kitchen. Of course, nothing had changed, Amy realized. What was different was how she was feeling about her life.

She moved to the kitchen and opened the refrigerator door, more from habit than from hunger. Nothing appealed to her, and she closed the door. Her laptop seemed to be glaring at her from the kitchen table. An unusual nervousness seemed to have taken her over; there was no comfort on her couch, and after moving to her favorite love seat, she found no ease there, either. It was disconcerting—she felt emotionally off balance, tense, as if she were waiting for news that she knew would be bad, painful, difficult to accept. She changed from her church clothes, not paying much attention to the jeans and shirt she put on. As she was coming down the stairs from her bedroom, she had an idea. "Why not?" she said aloud. She called Bobby to her, grabbed her purse, and went to her Jeep before she had time to change her mind.

There was never much traffic around Coldwater, and on Sundays even the farm vehicles and delivery trucks were absent. Amy had done lots of exploring when she first moved in—following roads to see where they led, stopping at roadside stands to buy vegetables or flowers, learning a bit about her new locale. She'd seen the sign she was looking for a couple of times in her wanderings, and she had a general idea of how to find it again. *Should I be doing this?* she wondered. Answering herself, she repeated the words she'd said at home: "Why not?"

A long, gradual curve to her left seemed familiar, and then, almost immediately, she saw the sign in the front yard. The house was an old one but well maintained, with crisp white paint and an inviting porch that extended the full length of the front of the house, complete with a pair of hanging gliders and three wicker rocking chairs. There was a small building to the rear about the size of a small barn. The lawn wasn't a lush green—none of them were at this time of year—but it was neatly trimmed. The long driveway wasn't paved but had been recently rolled and covered with a layer of crushed stone. There was a parking area next to the house, and then the driveway swung off to the front of the smaller structure.

Amy pulled into the parking area; her car was the only one there. She shut down her engine and listened for a few moments to the ticking of the cooling motor, wondering if anyone were home. Bobby excitedly sniffed the air through his few inches of open window. Amy opened her door and stepped out; Bobby followed the briefest part of a second later, brushing past her, standing with his head raised, tasting the air.

Zack greeted them before Ben did. Bobby's brother dashed around the side of the little barn and skidded to a stop in front of Bobby. There was none of the stiff-legged, raised-hackle sort of introduction older male dogs performed instinctively. Instead, the pups touched noses and looked one another over for a moment, at first tentatively. Then, Zack yipped and charged off across the grass, and Bobby followed right behind him. Together they charged a sparrow that'd been searching the lawn for insects; their puppy-barked challenges brought a smile to Amy's face. Ben, his hair, shirt, and jeans tan with a coating of sawdust, grinned and hurried his pace as soon as he saw her.

"Amy! Good to see you. What brings you out here on such a fine Sunday morning?" His smile was warm, welcoming—and very pleasantly surprised.

"I had to turn down your invitation earlier this week, and I'm sorry that I couldn't make it then. But I really wanted to see that sideboard you mentioned, so I wasn't doing anything after church and I thought . . . well . . ." Her words sounded a bit rapid to her own ears, and she felt heat in her face.

"I'm glad you're here. I was going to call again later on today." He held out his hand but started to withdraw it. "I'm all saw-dusty."

Amy took the offered hand and held it for a moment. His palm and the inside of his fingers were hard with calluses, but his grip was gentle and dry. "A little sawdust never hurt anyone," she said.

"C'mon," Ben said. "Let me show you my shop." He glanced over at the dogs, who were now rolling over one another in some sort of ferocious fake battle. "I see the guys have reunited. They'll run each other ragged. Good thing I just filled Zack's water dish—they'll need it." His eyes found Amy's. "I'm glad you stopped by."

She nodded. "Me too."

Ben's truck was backed up to the rear of the shop building, where a pile of large rough slabs of wood had been stacked. They went in a large side door. The air was hot in spite of a large pedestal fan and redolent with the fresh smell of sawdust. One of the slabs was resting on a pair of sawhorses.

"This is going to be the top of a table," Ben explained. "I've just started the rough sanding." He pointed toward the front of the building, where a tarp covered a project. "My sideboard," he said.

Ben lifted the tarp carefully and then stood back. Amy gasped. The piece was massive, with six large drawers, a long, broad top surface, and eight cupboards awaiting doors. "It's beautiful," Amy said.

"It's bird's-eye maple with walnut inlay," Ben told her. "The materials alone cost a fortune, but once I got started with it I couldn't back off. I've got the fittings on order, but there's a ton of finish work before I hang them."

Amy watched Ben as he spoke. He was completely un-self-conscious, in his glory describing something important to him, important to who he was. *Like Jake talking about his horses* . . . She chased the thought from her mind.

"Let's go to the kitchen where it's a bit cooler and have something to drink," Ben said.

"Sounds good. And will I meet your father? I've been looking forward to that."

"Sorry, Amy, not this time. My cousin picked Dad up for a birthday party. He won't be back until suppertime."

"Next time, then," Amy said.

The dogs were side by side in the shade of the house; they were both breathing heavily, with their tongues hanging out. "Little hot for more ripping around," Ben said. "How about if I put them in the storm cellar to cool down for a bit?" When Amy agreed, he called Zack, opened the storm cellar door, and motioned the dog inside. Bobby followed his brother. "There's water for them, and there's nothing they can get into. They'll be fine," he assured Amy.

The kitchen was cooler, and the iced coffee Ben served was tasty and refreshing. The conversation flowed easily, centered around their dogs at first and then moving on to more personal grounds.

"Why no wife and family, Ben?" Amy asked. "You seem like the type of guy who'd love that life."

"I probably would," Ben admitted. "I was pretty serious with a lady a couple of years ago." Some pain showed in his eyes. "It . . . didn't work out. She went off to work as a commercial artist at a big agency in Chicago. We talked about me following and opening a shop there—making cabinets and furniture. I went to Chicago." He paused for a long moment. "There was no way I could live there. Even in the suburbs I felt boxed in, as if there were too many people in too little space. I met some of Sandy's—that was her name—new friends. I didn't like them, and they didn't like me. So. Well . . . when I got back to Montana I wanted to get down and kiss the ground. And, here I am."

"Would your dad have gone with you—if you moved to Chicago, I mean?"

Ben grinned ruefully. "He said he'd rather live with a permanent toothache. He was going to move in with my cousin here if I left. What about you, Amy? Anyone in your life?"

Amy ran through a very abbreviated version of the story of Tom, the reconciliation, and the final breakup.

"Tough," Ben said. "I'm sorry."

"It was a long time ago." She smiled and added, "Kind of."

They discovered mutual likes and dislikes. They both enjoyed blues music, Snyder's pretzels, Red Delicious apples, poking around in antique stores and at flea markets. They agreed that there was no reason for cauliflower to exist anywhere in the universe.

It was after three when Amy gathered up her dog and Ben walked with them to her Jeep. "I'll call during the week," he said. "Maybe we can do something together—dinner or something."

"I'd like that," she said.

As soon as she got into her kitchen, Amy clicked the switch to activate the ringer on her telephone. She hadn't yet stepped away when it rang, startling her.

"Amy Hawkins."

"Amy, I'm so glad I caught you. I was trying earlier, and the phone just rang and rang. Then, I thought maybe there was something wrong with your phone, and I checked with the operator, but she said it was in operation. Anyway, I'm sorry to be calling you—"

"Julie?" Amy asked, barely recognizing her friend's voice because of her breathless, almost frantic tone. "What's the matter? You sound upset."

175

"I am upset, Amy. I know you told me at church you wanted to be left alone today, and now I'm bothering you like this, when you wanted some peace and quiet—"

"Julie, hush! Come on—you're not bothering me. Tell me what's the matter, and tell me what I can do to help."

Amy heard Julie draw a long, shaky breath. "You're the only one I could think of, Amy. The other reporter at the *News-Express* is on vacation in Hawaii, and there's no one available to cover for me. I even called Brad, the sports guy, but he's at the Porterville rodeo until tonight, and by then it'll be too late."

"Too late for what? Slow down, Julie. Tell me what's going on."

Julie still sounded close to tears, but she was able to slow her flood of words to a more natural pace. "OK. Here's the problem. I've been following a human-interest story for a couple of months now. It's about a local boy who's going to achieve the status of Eagle Scout this evening at the Boy Scout investiture ceremony at the Chamber of Commerce building in town. His name's Will Bennett. He has a degenerative spinal disease, and he's in a wheelchair. But the attitude of this kid—he's seventeen—is just amazing. To be an Eagle Scout has been his lifelong ambition, even after he was diagnosed and put in a chair. He's fulfilled all the requirements he possibly could from his wheelchair, and the Scout council recognized that he deserves Eagle Scout status, so they decided to grant it to him, regardless of his handicap."

"That's wonderful, Julie. Will sounds like a great kid. But

176

what's the problem? You said the council is ready to bring him in, right?"

"They are. But I can't be there to cover the story. I promised Will and his parents and the rest of the Scouts and Will's teachers and just everyone in town that I'd be there to write about the ceremony. And now . . ."

"Why can't you be there? Has something happened to you or to Danny?"

"No, we're fine. It's a . . . family emergency. I can't go into it right now, but because of it, I can't go to the investiture." She drew a deep breath. "You're the only real writer I know—the only real writer in Coldwater who doesn't already work for the paper."

"Oh, Julie . . ."

"I mean it, Amy. To a pro like you, covering something like this will be child's play. Really. I only need maybe 750 words—900 at the outside. There'll be a *News-Express* photographer there. And you can get more background from him. He'll have the two pieces I've already done on Will with him too. Will you do it for me, Amy? The meeting's at 6:30 tonight."

Julie's heart was in her voice. Amy didn't stop to consider her response. "Of course I will, Julie. But I'm concerned about you and your emergency. Is there anything else I can do?"

"Oh, Amy, thanks so much. Don't worry about me. I mean it. I just can't go into it right now, but Danny and I have to leave town for a couple of days. I'll tell you all about it when I get back. And thanks again." Relief and joy were all but palpable in Julie's voice.

"Well . . . sure. No problem. You and Danny have a safe trip, and don't you worry about anything here."

After she hung up the phone, Amy wandered back outside. She'd been keeping an eye on Bobby through the door window as she spoke with Julie and saw that he was now napping next to her lawn chair. She sat down.

What have I done? she wondered as the full realization of what she'd committed to struck her. *I haven't been able to write a coherent word in weeks,* she chided herself. *I'll destroy this story that's so important to Julie and to this boy, Will. Why didn't I tell Julie what was going on? She'd have found someone else. There must be someone in Coldwater capable of writing a few words about a gutsy kid. Maybe even one of the boy's parents, or what about an English teacher from the high school? It wasn't fair of Julie to ask me to step in and . . .*

She sat up straight in the lawn chair, suddenly angry with herself. *Not fair? What isn't fair is my even giving a second to that kind of thought! Don't friends help friends?*

She stood, woke Bobby, and led him into the kitchen, where she checked the clock. It was 4:20, giving her better than two hours until the meeting in town. The skirt and blouse she wore to church that morning, she decided, would be fine after a little touch up with her iron. A nice long shower would help relax her, and freshly shampooed hair always looked neat and businesslike. She had a fresh spiral pad in her desk in the den, and she'd bring the fancy Sheaffer fountain pen one of her writers had given her for Christmas a couple of years ago. She smiled. "I'm just like Lois Lane," she said to her dog.

≈≈

The Chamber of Commerce building was what residents of Coldwater delighted in referring to as "our skyscraper." A four-story brick structure built in the late 1950s, it had the architectural grace and appeal of an upended shoe box, but it served the community well and faithfully as a meeting place and headquarters for a number of diverse groups and organizations, from Alcoholics Anonymous to the Grange to Boy and Girl Scout chapters, as well as 4-H and the Montana Historical Society, Coldwater Office.

There were a couple of pickups and cars in the parking lot when Amy arrived at 6:10 p.m. Bobby had protested when Amy clicked the chain to his collar outside her garage, whining deep in his throat as if accusing Amy of desertion and other unspeakable cruelties. She had no idea how long the meeting would last, however, and was sure the puppy would be better off at home rather than waiting for her in the Jeep in a parking lot.

Amy locked her vehicle and, steno pad in hand, crossed the asphalt lot to the big double-door entrance. She felt almost barefoot in her low-heeled shoes; wearing boots had become a way of life for her. She smiled a bit at what she was feeling: a nervousness, an attack of butterflies in her stomach, that she hadn't experienced since she began her last major editing project with the writer of bestselling romance novels. *This will be good for me*, she thought. *I'll be doing a favor for a friend, I'll meet some new neighbors—and I'll write some words for publication. It's not my novel, but it's writing, and that's what I need to do. This might be a step in the right direction.*

The sensation that something was wrong—or at least different—tickled Amy's mind as she entered the building and began following the cardboard signs bearing the familiar Boy Scout symbol. She stopped in the hall for a moment, and then the sensation defined itself. *I'm going into a civic building, and there's no armed guard and no metal detector. No one waved a techno-wand over my body, and no one pawed through the contents of my purse.* It was a good feeling, a small thing perhaps, but something that made her once again glad she'd moved to Coldwater.

The auditorium had about a hundred seats that faced a stage with a central podium and a long table placed ten feet behind it. Amy introduced herself to a white-haired man who was fiddling with a microphone at the podium.

"I'm Amy Hawkins," she said. "I'm here for Julie Pulver and the *News-Express.* Julie couldn't make it . . ."

The man extended his hand. "I hope Julie's not ill or something?"

"No, nothing like that. She'd been looking forward to this."

"We all have. This is a big occasion for the boys and their families." He nodded back at the table. "Just take a seat, Amy. The others will be along shortly. Oh, I'm Charlie Derwick, by the way. I'm the MC."

"I don't need to be up here, Charlie," Amy protested. "I'll find a seat in the audience."

"Nonsense." Charlie smiled. "As I said, this is a big deal

for us. We'd like the press represented and visible, along with the others at the table. Go on now—make yourself comfortable."

Amy smiled graciously. "I'll be glad to," she said. "Thanks." Feeling a tad self-conscious, Amy walked to the table and took the end seat. The auditorium was beginning to fill, and the buzz of conversation increased. Two men, both Boy Scout officials in full uniform, and a pair of women, the town historian and the assistant to the mayor, joined Amy. Introductions were made, and Amy fielded questions about Julie, assuring the others that there was no real problem—simply a conflict in scheduling. The mayor of Coldwater was the last to be seated at the table.

The ceremony started precisely on time. The new Eagle Scouts were good-looking young men, Amy thought. Clear-eyed and straight-backed, they stood at attention as their names were called to step up and receive the honor they were there for.

The rubber tires of Will Bennett's wheelchair squeaked on the polished floor as he rolled to center stage and shook the hand of the master of ceremonies. Then, he spoke, holding the microphone a little too close to his face. "Sorry," he said as a squeal of static jolted the audience. His words, quite obviously memorized, were nevertheless honest and compelling.

"I don't want to be thought of as the guy in the wheel-chair," he said. "I want to be thought of as the Eagle Scout. That's more important than the way I get around these days . . ."

Amy scratched a few key words on the first page of her pad, knowing that what she'd seen and heard and stored away in her mind would be more important to the story than the quick impressions she registered at the time. The applause for Will Bennett was, of course, thunderous. Amy spoke to the young man and his parents afterward, explained Julie's absence, and learned more about young Will. He was, she decided, exactly what he seemed to be: a kid who'd had a lousy break but had survived it and was making a life for himself. He told her he wanted to be a science teacher. Amy could see him at age twenty-five or so, with at least a master's degree behind him, rolling into a classroom of enthusiastic kids. It was a good picture. Amy was certain she could write about what she was thinking and convey it to Julie's readers. *Or—to my readers?*

There was still some sunlight as Amy drove home from the Chamber building, but the light was soft and the few clouds at the western horizon seemed to be sinking with the sun.

Bobby had stepped in or otherwise upended his water dish and had tossed his toy a foot beyond the reach that his chain afforded him, so he was more than usually ecstatic to see Amy. She unclipped the chain and watched the pup, smiling as he ran off almost three hours of stored-up energy. The puppy raced in circles, barked at nothing, dashed back to Amy, and then took off again. When his tongue was hanging out and he was breathing hard from his frolic, Amy led him into the house. It was a few minutes after nine o'clock. She had no idea what time Jake would get back from Porterville.

Nutsy wound his way between her feet as she stood at the kitchen counter and put a filter, coffee, and water into her Mr. Coffee. She picked the cat up and sat at the kitchen table, cuddling him. His purring sounded as loud as a chain saw in the stillness of the house.

"Poor Nutsy," she said to him, scratching under his chin, a favorite spot of the cat's. "Don't you forget that you were here first—that Bobby came after you. You were the first one in my heart." Nutsy writhed in her arms. She lowered her head and nuzzled him, breathing in the clean scent of his coat, feeling the vibration of his almost ecstatic purring. It was a good moment and too soon over.

The Mr. Coffee began its "I'm ready" gurgling, and Bobby, jealous, pawed at her. Amy set Nutsy on the floor, checked the food and water bowls of both of her pets, poured a mug of coffee, and sat at the table behind her keyboard. She started the laptop and listened to its whirs and snaps until the system was ready. She shut down the page of her novel that appeared on the screen, opened a new document, and centered on the blank screen the title she'd decided upon during the drive home: "An Evening of Honor—A Young Man's Dream Fulfilled." The cursor pulsed at the beginning of the line that would begin the text. She drank from her cup and then set it aside.

The cursor continued its perfectly synchronized blinking.

Nothing happened. The impressions of the evening, the bits and parts of it that had touched Amy, were still present, but the words she needed to describe them to readers didn't appear on the screen. Her fingers were poised and ready to type, but there were no signals from her heart reaching them. She closed her eyes, seeing Will Bennett's face, seeing the love and pride in the eyes of his mother, hearing the applause for this singular teenager. No words came.

I am not going to allow this to happen. I will *write this little bit of an article.*

The squeak of the tires of Will's wheelchair against the floor was a visual and auditory impression Amy wanted to convey—how the tiny sound was loud in the hush of the auditorium, and how it was shared by all present. The image—the concept—had stayed with her since the very second it happened. It was the protest of a sneaker against a gym floor—something Will would never cause by himself. It was the smallest part of the evening, the most miniscule part of what she had experienced, yet it somehow represented as much as the speeches and the applause.

The words didn't come easily. She had to drag each one out of her mind as if they were nailed there. Sentences took forever; paragraphs much longer.

Shortly before midnight Amy had about eight hundred words. She printed out her work, sat back in her chair, and looked at her opening line and first paragraph.

> The squeal of a sneaker on the polished surface of a
> high school gymnasium floor as he makes a fast break
> toward the hoop is a sound that Will Bennett will
> never generate. He won't swing casually aboard a horse

as so many Coldwater young people do, and he won't experience the first-love closeness of dancing with his girlfriend at the senior prom. He will, however, wear the uniform and insignia of an Eagle Scout as he sits in

She put the page down and rubbed her eyes with the heels of her hands. *A little over-the-top, maybe. A little too sweet, possibly. Still, the texture I want is there. It starts with what Will can't do and continues about what he can. That's a good, solid reader hook. A little tweaking, some more rewording, some tightening of a couple of paragraphs . . . It's not bad. It's not bad at all.*

She was surprised when she looked at the clock: 12:21. A memory—an unbidden one—flooded over her for no reason she could define. She was in her childhood bed, her face wet with tears, her body tight with fear, vestiges of a nightmare still very real in the shapes in the darkness of her bedroom. Her frantic crying, her panicked screams, her gasping for breath, were terribly loud in the night silence. Then, suddenly, the long aisle between her room and that of her parents was filled with light, and she heard her mother's slippers padding toward her room. She'd be safe. That wonderful surge of light promised her that. Everything would be all right. The bad things would be gone, chased back to wherever they'd come from.

The Bennett article, Amy realized, was synonymous with the light outside of her bedroom all those years ago. And that little piece of writing was as important to her right then as her mother's assurances had been thirty years ago. Amy held that thought, made certain that it'd become part of her.

Long-held tension and fear began to lose their stranglehold on her.

"Breakthrough," she said aloud.

Now there was the Jake Winter situation to deal with. It was too late for coffee, and anyway, the inch or so left in the Mr. Coffee carafe looked like watered-down tar. She poked around in a cupboard, found a box of various tea bags she'd collected over the years, put back a bag of Red Zinger, and selected one labeled "Sleepy Time." She ran water into her teakettle and put it on the stove.

She stretched again and considered an aspirin for the pain in her lower back. Her hands, too, she noticed, were vaguely sore, her fingers feeling a bit stiff. She picked up the pages of the article from the counter where she'd dropped them and walked to the kitchen table. Her laptop was still running, and the cursor still blinked at her. She switched the machine off and placed the night's work next to it. She looked at the clock again: 12:36. The water on the stove began to boil. She turned off the burner and poured the water over the tea bag in a mug, which she set aside as being too hot to drink immediately. She called Bobby and walked with him out the back door and into the yard.

As the dog ran out to his favorite spot, Amy peeked around the edge of her garage across the pasture to Jake's place. The dull gleam of the stock truck near the metal building told her Jake had gotten back from Porterville.

When he'd returned, she had no idea. She hadn't heard a thing as she worked.

Just as well, she thought, not really believing it. *If he doesn't come over, there won't be an argument, and I won't have to listen to some lame explanation of why he and Mallory were so cozy together.* Amy walked closer to the fence. Voices reached her across the distance. They were male voices, she could tell that, but couldn't make out actual words. Hooves clattered on the floor of the truck, and a horse snorted loudly. Then the hooves made a more hollow sound as a horse was led down the stock truck's ramp.

Must've just gotten in—they're unloading the horses. Amy couldn't really see anything but the top of the big truck, but she stood in the cool air and watched until Bobby nosed at her, ready to go inside for the night. She drank her tea in the kitchen, washed the empty mug with unusual thoroughness, and set it on the rack to dry. Both animals' water dishes were full. There were no other dishes to clean and nothing else in the kitchen that needed to be done. Still, she stood at the counter, not reaching to turn off the light that showed she was home and awake and in her kitchen.

This is stupid. I'm tired. I should be in bed. I don't know why I'm standing here like a manikin in a store window. She walked into the living room, leaving the light on in the kitchen, feeling foolish but unable to head upstairs to bed quite yet. She picked up an advertising circular from the coffee table and sat down to page through it. First she clicked on the floor lamp. The brochure extolled the glories of replacement storm windows for older homes. Her own windows—and

187

her entire home, for that matter—were barely six months old. She read the ad copy as if it held the secret of life.

Ten minutes later she tossed the circular aside and stood, switched off the lamp, and went to the kitchen to extinguish the light in there before going up the stairs to her bedroom.

It was then that the light tapping sounded from her door. "Amy," Jake's voice called quietly, not much louder than a whisper. "You still up?"

8

Amy clicked on the lamp in the living room, paused for a moment, and eased the door open.

"Jake," she said noncommittally.

"I know it's awful late, but I just got in and unloaded the stock and . . . well . . . I needed to talk to you. I saw your kitchen light on, and I figured you might still be up."

"I worked late tonight," Amy said. "Something I needed to get finished." They stood two feet apart for a long moment. Even in the murky light from the single lamp in the living room that filtered into the entryway, Amy could see that Jake looked tired—and a bit scruffy. His hair was windblown, the Western shirt he wore needed a trip through the washing machine, and a shave wouldn't have hurt his appearance, either. He even smelled a bit gamey: not bad, necessarily, but of work and horses and road dust. Actually, she admitted to herself, the scent was masculine and out-doorsy and not really unpleasant. She swung the door open wider and said, "Come on in. There's no sense in standing out here to talk."

Amy led Jake into the living room and turned on the

overhead light as she passed the switch plate on the wall. She sat in a love seat facing the couch. "Sit," she said. "I have some iced tea, if you'd like something to drink."

"No thanks. I won't stay long." He brushed at the back of his jeans and then sat on the couch.

"How was the rodeo?" Amy asked.

For a brief bit of time the fatigue left Jake's eyes, and a smile began to form on his face. "It went very well. My bull—Little Butterball is his name—wasn't ridden to the buzzer once all weekend. He's looking real good. And one of the guys drew a ninety-three riding my bronc Locoweed. This kid from Hidden Falls put a great ride on him, had the crowd on their feet."

"That's good. I'm glad it went well for you."

"Yeah. Thanks."

An uncomfortable silence settled into the room in the same manner storm clouds invade a sunny day. Jake shifted on the couch and leaned forward, hands clasped on his knees. "I guess you don't really want to hear about the rodeo right now," he said.

Amy didn't reply.

"I heard you were in Porterville early yesterday. Wade told me he saw you." He waited a beat. "You didn't stay for the show."

"No. I mean, yes, I was there, but no, I didn't stay."

"I . . . yeah. I see."

Amy breathed an exasperated sigh. "Look, Jake, this isn't necessary. I think I misunderstood some things that I shouldn't have. I made an assumption that was silly and that I shouldn't have made. I thought—well, what I thought doesn't make any difference. Let's just forget the whole thing and get back to being neighbors."

Jake's eyes found hers. "Is that what you want, Amy?"

A quick flicker of anger arose in Amy, making her words sound harder than normal. "Look," she said, "let's quit dancing around this, OK? The time we spent together meant something to me."

"It was important to me too, Amy. It meant that we were becoming close to one another, that it was good for us to be together, that—"

"Maybe I was thinking too fast and too far ahead, Jake. It seems to me that Mallory is very important to you, and not just as a trainer. I saw you and Mallory kissing at your trailer at the rodeo."

Jake looked stunned. "What're you . . . I don't get it, Amy. Mallory? What are you talking about? Where did all this come from?"

Amy shook her head. "I was just beyond the trailer Saturday morning when you and Mallory came out of it, Jake—with your arms around each other, laughing like a pair of . . . I don't know what."

"You have it all wrong, Amy. What you saw wasn't what you thought it was." His words were urgent, his voice tight and louder now. "You're jumping to a conclusion that isn't based on what's real. And you're not giving me a chance to explain what you saw."

"You don't owe me an explanation. I have no claim on you, or you on me. What you do with your time or whom you spend it with is totally up to you."

"You're wrong, Amy," Jake interrupted. "You've taken one little moment and built it up into some great conspiracy against you, and you're not willing to hear me out, to give me the chance to tell you what really happened Saturday."

"OK, then," Amy said quietly. "Why don't you tell me about what I saw? If I'm so wrong, tell me why I'm wrong."

She saw how his throat moved as he swallowed hard once, and then again, before speaking. "First of all," he said, "Mal Powers works for me—she's my employee. She trains horses and she does other things too. Such as helping out at rodeos where I've taken my stock, just like Wade or Wes or any of the other people I pay every two weeks."

Amy began to respond, but Jake held up his hand, his eyes showing fire now. "Wait. Second, Mallory was staying at the boardinghouse in Porterville where the rodeo committee put up those who weren't pulling trailers and didn't have places to stay. She came to my trailer Saturday morning because there was no hot water left at the boardinghouse—some kind of a plumbing malfunction—and she was all grubby from feeding my stock and cleaning the animals up to get them ready for the first show. She asked if she could use the shower."

"And you—"

"And I," Jake interrupted again, "went over to the coffee stand while she was in the trailer. I brought back coffee and called in to her, asking if she was decent. When she said she was, I went in. We drank our coffee, and she said she needed to get back to the holding pens, and I had a million things to do at the chutes and with the contestants. We must have just been leaving the trailer when you saw us." He paused. "That's all there was to it."

"That's not exactly what I saw, Jake," Amy said. "Mallory was cozied up next to you. She kissed you on the cheek. And I didn't notice you having any problems with that."

Jake exhaled a long breath. He tensed; Amy could see he was about to stand up. "I guess you've already made up your mind," he said. "That you're flat-out wrong doesn't make any difference to you, right?"

"How am I wrong? Tell me that, Jake."

Again he exhaled loudly. He broke eye contact, and instead of looking at her face he concentrated on his hands clutched together on his knees. "Look, Mallory is kind of . . . Well, she's had a . . . a thing for me for a few years—ever since I first met her, actually. She'd flirt with me constantly. She'd even call on the phone, late at night, every so often. All that stopped over two years ago. Then, recently, she wrote to me telling me how well she was doing with cutting horses and outlining how well I could do with a trainer like her here on my ranch. I was already very interested in cutting horses. The market for them is huge. I talked with her a few times, and she seemed like she was all business. There was no more nonsense." He looked at Amy again. "So, I hired her. Maybe I was wrong. But I didn't do it because I was looking for a girlfriend. When I met you . . ."

"When you met me, what?" Amy asked.

"You were . . . *Special* is such a dumb word, but that's

what you were. I was ... well ... attracted to you. I liked your intelligence and your sense of humor and the way you'd left a different kind of life behind you." Several moments passed. Then, Jake added, "Ya know?" bringing a transient half smile to Amy's face.

"But what about what I saw at the trailer, Jake? What about that? If there's nothing romantic between you and Mallory, what was all the touchy-feely stuff and the laughter?"

"The touch-feely was on her part, no? Did you see me reach out to her at all? I'm sure you didn't. And what was I supposed to do? Hit her with a stick because she put an arm around my waist? Gave me a peck on the cheek? Because she made me laugh?" He stood and looked down at her. "Believe what you want, Amy. But what I've said is the truth."

Amy stood from the love seat.

"Seems to me that you've got a lot to think about," Jake said. "Like whether or not I'm playing some kind of devious game with you and your feelings. I guess right now isn't the best time to talk about it. You need some time to take a good, close look at what you think happened Saturday, and what I've told you actually happened. So, why don't you do that? Think about it, I mean?"

His hand began to move out to her and then dropped back to his side. There was some pain in his eyes, she thought, but no sign of duplicity. "Tomorrow morning about nine I'm going out riding," he said. The beginning of a smile creased his face. "I'll have Daisy all saddled up. I thought I'd come by here before I went out. If you were inclined to climb up on the ol' gal, well, we could maybe ride some and talk some more."

"I don't know, Jake . . ."

His grin grew larger. "Whatever. I'll be here at nine, either way. If you don't want to go riding, I guess I'll turn ol' Daisy over to the Alpo folks. Seems a shame, though."

Amy couldn't hold back her laugh. Before she could say anything, Jake was moving to the entryway. "I'll be by at nine," he said, closing the door behind him.

Amy stood in place, dazed, not at all sure of what had just taken place. Then she realized she still had a smile on her face and felt better than she had in a couple of days. *There'd be no advantage for him to lie about all of this*, she told herself. *If he had feelings for Mallory, he probably wouldn't have come here at all tonight—he'd just let the whole thing drop. There are men who need to play one woman off another, but I can't believe that of Jake Winter.* She went into the kitchen and turned off the light, catching the lamp and overhead in the living room as she headed for the stairs. Nutsy was asleep on her pillow when she reached her bedroom, and Bobby flopped down on the throw rug next to the bed as Amy undressed and pulled on her nightgown. She looked into her own eyes as she brushed her teeth in the bathroom.

I've learned a lot about people in the course of my life. I think I know whom I can trust and who isn't worthy of trust. She recalled a couple of men she'd briefly dated and cringed. *Maybe it's having been exposed to losers like them that makes me so suspicious, so unwilling to accept good things and good people.* She didn't realize how long she'd been standing there mechanically brushing until she looked away from her eyes in the mirror and down to her mouth. Toothpaste froth frosted her lips and made her look rabid.

It was too late to read. Amy turned off the lamp on her bedside table without touching the novel she'd started a couple of nights ago. She settled into her bed, tucked the covers around herself, and closed her eyes. She was drifting into the mindless warmth of the first stages of sleep when a thought jarred her, and her eyes popped open.

What about Ben Callan? The hours she'd spent with him had been pleasurable—easy, fun, interesting—and more. Perhaps much more. *I wouldn't have gone to his home if I didn't feel some attraction to him, didn't feel something more than a passing friendship. He's bright and sensitive and . . . well . . . cute. And kind—he brought Bobby to me, knowing without discussing it with me how I'd fall in love with the puppy.* She pushed herself to a sitting position and leaned back against the headboard, staring out into the darkness of her bedroom. Nutsy, his sleep disturbed by her movements, stretched, yawned, and settled back down. Bobby, on the throw rug next to the bed, stirred for a moment but didn't awaken.

Was I too quick to accept what Jake said tonight? He left knowing I'd go riding with him tomorrow, and it was clear to both of us, even though we didn't actually say so, that a reconciliation has already taken place between us. And nothing short of the end of the world could keep me from being ready when Jake shows up with his horses tomorrow morning.

Amy's confusion manifested itself physically. She felt her shoulder muscles tighten. *Of course I feel something for*

Jake Winter. But it's equally true that I feel something for Ben Callan too. I've never been able to spend time with more than one man—never wanted to, either. So, what do I do now?

By eight the next morning Amy was showered, dressed, breakfasted, and sipping at her second mug of coffee. It was, again, a typical Montana summer morning: a crystal clarity to the coolish air, the sky an almost incredibly deep shade of blue just short of indigo, and a sun that promised heat later in the day. Amy hummed as she rinsed her cereal bowl and spoon and placed them on the drying rack on the counter next to the sink. Both her animals were fed, and she'd walked with Bobby into the scrub and dirt beyond her property.

Her laptop glared at her from the kitchen table, and she did her best to avoid looking at it—to avoid even thinking about it or recognizing that it was there waiting for her. Her Bennett article was placed in a clasp envelope with the name of the editor—Nancy Lewis—that Julie had given her, ready to be dropped at the *News-Express* as soon as she returned from riding with Jake. After that there'd be plenty of time to wrestle with her novel.

Amy busied herself—killed time, actually—being domestic. She straightened whatever she could find to straighten, sifted through her mail, separated the junk, and dropped it, unopened, into her recycling box. She dusted her bookshelves and tables and suffered through a few minutes of the roar of her old vacuum as she ran it over the living room carpet. At quarter to nine she sat on the couch and paged through a new copy of *Writer's Digest*, waiting to hear the sound of

Jake's horses as he came up the driveway. At precisely nine she heard the rumble of a truck and stepped to the picture window. A two-horse trailer with a pair of horse rear ends and tails showing eased up toward the house. Jake stopped his pickup, set the parking brake, and stepped out just as Amy left her house. "What's with the trailer?" she asked as she approached Jake.

"Special trail ride today," he said with a grin. "C'mere." Amy walked closer, and Jake pointed at a large Igloo cooler in the bed of the truck. "There's a picnic in there—sandwiches, drinks, chips, a piece of cheese, all kinds of stuff."

"Sounds wonderful. But Jake, we were going to talk. Remember?"

"We will, Amy. I promise. But for right now, let's get going."

"Where are we going?"

"You get another Montana history lesson today," Jake said. "There's a sort of a ghost town an hour or so off the road not too far from here. Cuylerville it was called. It was a stage depot for a few years after a vein of gold was discovered. When the vein was all worked out, the town just kinda withered away. There're still some buildings standing—a saloon, a storefront, parts of a little church. If you like, we can scrounge around for artifacts. I picked up an old pocketknife and a dinner plate—well, most of a dinner plate—the last time I was there."

"Wow!" Amy exclaimed. "I love stuff like that. Hey, I've got a little camera. Can I bring it along?"

"Sure, grab it and let's go."

Amy started toward her house and then stopped and turned back. "Are we going through town? Past the *News-Express* building?"

"We go right past it to swing onto the old main road," Jake said.

"Great—if we can stop for a minute, I have something I need to drop off. OK? I could email it, but I'm kinda superstitious—I'd like to hand the piece over rather than send it through cyberspace."

"Sure, no problem. Like I said, we're going right past it."

When they got into town, Jake pulled up directly in front of the big glass main entry doors at the *News-Express*, and Amy dashed in with her envelope, leaving it with the receptionist. When she climbed back into the truck, Jake had put a tape into the player—Bonnie Raitt.

"I always liked her," Amy said. "Is she still singing?"

"I dunno. This tape is older than dirt, but it still plays just fine." He pulled onto the road and accelerated. "I can't say much for pop music these days," he said. "That hip-hop idiocy is nothing but noise, and the lyrics would make a buffalo hunter blush."

"Yeah," Amy agreed, "I can't stand that stuff." She leaned forward to raise the volume a bit—and moved a few inches closer to Jake. He noticed her move and took his hand from the shift lever and reached for hers. She fit her palm to his. They held hands until Jake needed to shift again.

They rode in silence for several miles, Jake keeping slightly below the speed limit because of the horse trailer he pulled.

When he reached over again to take her hand, Amy smiled. "Let's talk, OK?"

"Sure. You start."

"Now, there's a great way to kill a conversation before it even gets going."

"Sorry." Jake's tone indicated that he actually was sorry. "I turned everything over and around in my mind last night after I left your place. I don't know what words I can say that will tell you how . . . how I feel about you. I decided that the best thing I can do is answer any questions about Mallory or anything else as honestly as I can."

Amy had to take a deep breath. Jake's "how I feel about you" had made her feel that suddenly all the oxygen had left the cab of the truck. "I was confused, Jake—confused and hurt. When I saw you and Mallory at Porterville, the way you seemed so involved with one another, how good you seemed together, it made me believe that you'd lied to me. I'm an old-fashioned girl."

"I guess I could see that about you right from the start, Amy. It's a big part of what attracted me to you. See, I'm old-fashioned too. My folks had the most wonderful and loving marriage in the world. I decided early on that I didn't have to settle for anything less than that."

Amy let a moment pass. "Your parents—they're both gone?"

"Yeah. For a few years now. They married late in life and had me late. I don't have sisters or brothers. My dad died of lymphatic cancer, and it seemed like my mom couldn't live without him. She died a couple years later."

"I'm sorry," Amy said.

"They both had good lives, and they gave me a good life. There wasn't much money, but we had the ranch—the same place I own now. When they bought the place, land was at almost giveaway prices. My dad ran some cattle, some horses." He squeezed Amy's hand slightly. "What about your family?"

"Both my parents are alive. They live in Connecticut. They're both retired. They travel quite a bit. I'm an only child, just like you."

Jake seemed to be waiting for more. When Amy didn't go on, he asked, "Are you close to them?"

"I love them both, and they love me," she answered honestly. "But we have totally different value systems and perspectives. They thought I was nuts for moving to Montana, for instance. My mom's sure all Montana men chew tobacco, drink corn liquor, and carry guns."

"Some do." Jake chuckled. "You've described some of the cowhands I've had working for me." He waited a beat. "So, you're not close?"

"No. There's love between us, but not . . . I don't know . . . warmth. Or understanding."

A comfortable silence began. Amy leaned back, closed her eyes, and drifted with her thoughts. When Jake downshifted, and she felt him turning to the right shoulder, she opened her eyes and looked around her. "Are we there?" she asked.

Jake stopped the truck and set the hand brake. Amy looked out the window. There was nothing but prairie—no fences, no signs, no ranches—in all directions. She turned to him quizzically.

"No, we're not there yet. But I had to stop. I kept glancing over at you after you closed your eyes." He unsnapped his shoulder harness and moved closer to Amy. "I . . . well . . ." he mumbled as he took her in his arms.

Amy waited for his kiss, wanting it, loving the spontaneity of it—and grinning inwardly at his little-boy shyness. His lips were warm on hers, and she inhaled his scent, the clean, masculine fragrance that seemed to emanate from him. It was a gentle kiss with no urgency to it, and they both reveled in it for a long moment. "Whew," Jake said as he moved back behind the wheel.

"Whew," Amy agreed.

The ghost town was about an hour and a half ride on horseback from where Jake parked the truck and trailer. There was no road—not even a path—to follow. When they were out of sight of the truck, Amy felt as if she and Jake were in their own universe; the total population consisted of two humans and two horses. She told Jake about it.

"Not a bad world, Amy," he said. "I'd go there in a second."

Daisy, the same bay mare Amy had ridden when she and Jake visited the Indian burial mounds, was her mount again today. The horse did her job admirably with no arguing or fractiousness, giving Amy a most pleasant ride.

The few buildings that stood in Cuylerville were gray

and tired and leaned sharply away from the prevailing wind, looking like each minute would be their last. Daisy stumbled over a wagon rut but easily recovered. "This would have been the main street," Jake said. "A mud pit in the spring and winter and a dust bowl during the summer." He pointed to a pile of warped, desiccated lumber and crumbling bricks. "That was the church, I think." He swung his arm in the other direction, at a two-car-garage-sized building, only the front and one side of which were standing—and those precariously. "That was the saloon. I know that because there are lots of broken whiskey bottles scattered around inside it."

Amy was fascinated; she tugged the camera from the pocket of her jeans and fitted her hand through its carrying cord. "Can we tie the horses and poke around a bit?" she asked. "I want to get pictures of all this."

A few trees baked in the sun not far beyond where the church had once stood. They provided minimal shade but at least would keep the horses from the direct assault of the sun. "Over there," Jake said. "Then we can poke around all you like."

Amy found the cover and a few pages of a book of hymns under some boards in the church. In the saloon Jake dug out a cup that was almost whole except for a nick in its rim. The treasure of the day was a serving spoon Amy found while grubbing through the ruins of what they decided had been a general store.

They stood in the center of the street as Amy clicked off her final snapshots.

"You've really enjoyed this, haven't you?" Jake said. "You're like a kid in a candy store, digging around in all this junk."

"It's a wonderful place," Amy answered. "It's like a skeleton of the Old West, in a sense. If I close my eyes, I can see wagons and men on horseback and barefoot kids and ladies with parasols walking up and down the street, raising dust and going about their business."

Jake put his arm around Amy's waist. She flashed on the image of him with Mallory and her arm around his waist, but she quickly dismissed the thought. "You got quite an imagination," Jake said.

They walked back to the horses hand in hand, listening to the silence of the ghost town, savoring the time they were spending together exploring not only Cuylerville but a new relationship.

They rode back to the trailer and loaded the horses on it. Then Jake drove down the road a few more miles to a spot where a small stream cut through a stand of trees. Amy carried the blanket and a pair of plastic buckets to carry water back to the horses, and Jake carried the cooler. They arranged their picnic in the speckled shade quite close to the stream. The heat of the day was fully on them, its presence heavy and pervasive, but the mellifluous whisper of the water over the rocks in the streambed created an aura of gentle coolness.

Their conversation followed no particular fashion, and there were periods when no words were said for several minutes as they ate their sandwiches, drank their icy-cold tea, and enjoyed the perfect little oasis. Only once was the quiet intruded upon. Engine roar and the screech of tires scrambling for traction on the hot pavement from out on the road seemed as out of place there by the stream as a circus calliope would have been. Amy looked questioningly at Jake.

"Kids drag racing or something, I suppose," he said. He smiled. "You know—to impress a girlfriend."

Amy grinned. "Kind of like taking a girl to a ghost town and then on a picnic by a stream, right?"

"Exactly. And it's working, isn't it?"

She reached for his hand. "It's working perfectly."

Amy packed the scraps into the cooler while Jake was carrying the buckets of water back to the trailer. She sat on the blanket and tugged off her boots and socks and rolled her jeans up to her knees. The stream water was startlingly cold, and the bottom silty and littered with pebbles and larger pieces of rock and stone. The quick chill that ran the length of Amy's spine felt wonderful in contrast to the ovenlike heat that had settled in. Minnows zipped about in the clear water, at first frightened away but then returning to get a better look at Amy's feet. A piece of rusted metal protruded from the mud on the other side of the stream, and Amy crossed to it, placing her feet carefully to avoid the slippery larger rocks. She tugged at the edge of the object, and with a slurpy, sucking sound, a shallow pan—most of its bottom corroded away—came free.

"Looks like some old dreamer was panning for gold here a

hundred or so years ago," Jake said from shore. Amy started at his voice. She turned around to face him.

"I wonder if he found any nuggets, if he ended up rich," she mused.

Jake laughed. "He'd probably been just as well off panning in his bathtub. Looks like whoever he was, he wandered too far away from where the gold was to make any money."

Amy liked her own version of history better. "That doesn't mean that this fellow didn't come upon a whole bunch of it right here, loaded up his pockets and his horse, and chucked his pan away because he knew he was rich beyond his wildest dreams."

"His mule," Jake corrected. "Panners used mules as pack animals, not horses."

"This guy used a horse," Amy insisted. "He built a fine mansion, married the lady of his dreams, and lived happily ever after."

She turned when he touched her shoulder. "Sometimes people find gold nuggets when they're not even looking for them, you know." There was something in his eyes she'd never seen there before, something that made her heart swell in her chest. "I have, so I know that's true," he went on. "I thought I was falling in love with you. That's the wrong tense. The falling part is over and done with. I love you, Amy."

She moved into his embrace, feeling the strength in his arms and the slightest tremble in his chest. The words were difficult to say, but they were liberating, wondrous, tremendously honest words. "I love you too, Jake Winter."

Amy had noticed many times that euphoria didn't tend to last for long in her life. She was still drifting behind the sweet memories of her time with Jake when her telephone rang and Lloyd Sturgiss's voice brought her back to the real world.

"I'm just checking in with my favorite new literary icon," the agent said with a chuckle. "I completely realize that writers can hit snags, and that deadlines can seem oppressive when the ideas aren't flowing for whatever reason. I don't want to put any more pressure on you—that isn't why I called. My purpose here is to find out if there's anything I can do to help you through this dry spell. That's part of my job, you know. I have faith in you and in *The Longest Years*. You know that, right?"

"I do know that, Lloyd. You've been great."

"Thanks. But if there's anything I can do, you let me know. In the meantime, I'll get in touch with Meadow-dale. They're good to work with. I'll tell them we need a bit more time, is all. Believe me, this happens with a lot of books—particularly first novels."

"It's going to start rolling again, Lloyd—I know it is. If you can buy us that extra time, that would be great."

"Consider it done, Amy. No sweat. Now, what else do you need from me?"

"I can't think of a single thing, Lloyd. Really. But I appreciate the offer and your concern."

"Sure. Look, Amy, give me a call every so often, let me know how it's going, OK? And don't worry about anything here in the Big Apple."

"OK. I'll be in touch. Bye, Lloyd."

Amy stood at the telephone after the call was completed and looked over at the table across the kitchen from her. She started toward it, stopped, and veered off to the refrigerator. She hadn't eaten since the picnic with Jake, and she was suddenly voraciously hungry. She built a large and sloppy sandwich from bologna, lettuce, and several slices of Swiss cheese, and spread Roquefort salad dressing liberally over the ingredients before topping the mess with a second slice of bread. She sagged into a love seat and, with a plate and a wad of paper toweling in her lap, watched the shadows stretch across the wall.

Lloyd's a gem—and I owe both him and the publisher a book. I know that—and I also know I'll deliver the novel, and that it'll be a darn good story. A quick swing of mental images brought a smile to her face. *The time with Jake was wonderful. There could be something happy and enduring starting for both of us.*

9

Amy was up early the next morning, but in spite of the few hours of sleep she'd gotten, she felt fresh, rested, ready to meet the day. By seven o'clock she'd fed her animals, accompanied Bobby on his morning walk, and washed and dried her breakfast dishes—as usual, a bowl, a spoon, and a juice glass. Her laptop seemed to eye her from the kitchen table as she went about her morning chores, but it no longer intimidated her.

She'd noticed that Jake's mares were grazing placidly in the pasture when she went out with Bobby. Things began early at Jake's, she knew; the mares were turned out just before first light by half-asleep cowboys. Amy took her second cup of coffee outside and stood at the corner of her garage, watching the mares and enjoying the peace of the morning. The rain the night before had scrubbed the world clean, and everything around her seemed to sparkle with new life. That reminded her. Her Jeep was a mess. Dust-coated and unkempt, it hardly seemed like the vehicle she had anguished over before buying, planning a fanatical maintenance program to ensure that the SUV would still be in prime condition many years after her final payment was made.

She stepped into the garage and ran an index finger across the Jeep's rear gate, just below the rear window. Her finger came away grimy, and the finish had felt like sandpaper. "Car wash time," she said to Bobby. "And not just a hosing down in the driveway—the whole deal, the $6.95 Super Shine job in town."

She was loading Bobby into the passenger seat when she heard the telephone's insistent summons. After debating through a couple of rings, she dashed inside.

"Amy Hawkins," she answered.

"Amy," a businesslike female voice responded, "this is Nancy Lewis at the *News-Express*."

"Hi, Nancy," Amy said. "I hope the piece was all right. It'd been some time since I'd done any journalism, and I was a bit rusty."

"The story was terrific," Nancy said. "Very good—very professionally written. What I particularly liked was the approach. I know that you didn't know Will or his family, but a reader would think you'd been following the situation forever. That's good writing."

"Well . . . thanks," Amy said, nonplussed for a moment. "I'm glad it worked for you."

"It did. I'm wondering if you could stop by anytime today to talk for a minute. I'll be here chained to my desk all day, so whenever you can swing by is fine."

Amy grinned. It was obvious to her that Nancy Lewis wasn't accustomed to having invitations to meet with her turned down, that she made the automatic assumption that whomever she called would appear in her doorway soon. "I was just about to come into town," Amy said. "I can be there in fifteen or twenty minutes, if that works."

"Excellent. I'll see you shortly, then. The front desk will send you back to my office. I'll make sure they know you're coming."

Amy was about to respond when the connection was broken. *This lady is all business*, she mused. *No wonder Julie says she's such a strong editor and manager.* She looked down at her outfit after hanging up the telephone: boots, jeans, a sleeveless Western-style shirt. The jeans were fresh that morning, as was the shirt. For a moment Amy wondered about the propriety, wondered whether she should change into a skirt, and then decided against doing so. *This isn't a business meeting*, she thought, *and this is Coldwater, Montana, not Dallas or New York City*. She tugged a couple of sheets off the roll of paper towels on her counter, whisked some grit and blades of grass from her boots, and went back out into the garage.

The *News-Express* building was situated not far from the cluster of businesses—Drago's Café, Kornoelje's Bakery, the gas station/car wash, the Book Nook, the Bootery, and the other commercial operations that made up the town. Amy parked on the street, made certain that the Jeep's windows were cracked to provide Bobby some ventilation during his wait, locked her vehicle—a habit no one else in town seemed to bother with—and walked down the sidewalk to the large glass front doors of the newspaper.

211

As she approached the entrance she felt a not-unfamiliar thrumming—the vaguest sense of vibration—under the soles of her boots. The massive presses on which the *News-Express* was printed were located in a cavernous basement under the main building, and were in operation. Amy had visited production centers of major publishing houses in her editing career and had experienced the same sensation.

A cheery young receptionist took Amy's name and directed her on to Nancy Lewis's office on the first floor. Amy followed a long corridor from which offices and a series of cubicles branched. There was a businesslike buzz in the place, but whatever intensity existed was eased by the occasional bursts of laughter. Dress was casual at the *News-Express*; everyone, it seemed, wore boots rather than shoes, and the women wore pantsuits or slacks and blouses. The men favored clean jeans and short sleeved shirts. Ties were as rare as wingtip shoes.

The door marked "Nancy Lewis, Managing Editor" was half open. Amy tapped lightly on the frosted glass. The woman seated behind the large, old-fashioned wooden desk looked up at Amy and smiled. "Amy," she said in a slightly husky voice, "I'm Nancy. Our receptionist let me know you were on your way. Please come in—have a seat." She motioned toward an armchair positioned in front of her desk.

Amy smiled, crossed the room, and sat. "Good to meet you, Nancy," she said.

The editor appeared to be in her midfifties. Her hair was shoulder length, brown with a good amount of undisguised silver. She wore a tan business suit and a white, frilly-collared blouse. Amy found it almost impossible to imagine Ms. Lewis in jeans or shorts or a sweatshirt. Except for a single file in front of her on the polished surface, her desk was clear of all but a telephone and a yellow legal pad off to one side.

"Coffee, Amy?" Nancy asked. "It's the one luxury I allow myself here—Jamaican beans, freshly ground."

"Sounds good," Amy said. "Please."

Nancy picked up her telephone receiver, said a few words Amy couldn't quite hear, and hung up. "Again, thanks for the good work on such short notice."

Amy nodded. "I was glad to help Julie out. We haven't known one another long, but she's a special woman. The *News-Express* is fortunate to have her."

"And we realize that every day," Nancy said. "The thing is, we no longer have her—at least not for a while."

"Oh?" Amy asked.

"She's on a . . . well . . . a sabbatical for a few months, maybe longer."

The news stunned Amy. "A sabbatical? Is she sick? Is there something wrong? She loves her work here."

"No." Nancy smiled. "Nothing like that—not at all. I'm really sorry to leave you in the dark, but I'm sure Julie will be in touch with you later today. She'll fill you in on what's going on." She paused. "I'd dearly love to tell you more, but I gave her my word."

"I see," Amy said, not really seeing at all. "As long as she isn't ill . . ."

Nancy opened the file on her desk and glanced at the first page inside of it. Amy saw that the tab on the folder read "Hawkins, A." After a moment, Nancy closed the file. "I asked you here to offer you a job, Amy," she said.

"Whew," Amy breathed. "I have to admit that you've caught me by surprise."

"I'm sure I have. The thing is, with Julie out for some time and my other feature writer about to retire, I need someone to cover the local events and happenings in a way that'll draw and keep readers. Julie has that skill, and so do you. You'd be ideal in the position."

"That's very complimentary," Amy said. "But I'm not a journalist. If anything, I'm a novelist and an editor. And, I'm brand new to the Coldwater area. I don't have the contacts—the friends and acquaintances Julie has."

"I realize all that," Nancy said. "I took the liberty of Googling you before I asked you to come in. Your background is quite impressive." She smiled. "I think we both know that writing is writing, in a sense, whether it's news or pure fiction. And, from what Julie and a few other people have told me, you've fit in wonderfully in Coldwater. You'd develop sources and contacts with no problem."

Amy held eye contact but didn't respond immediately.

"You'd have time to work on your novel, Amy, and you'd have a paycheck coming in every two weeks." She named a figure. "That's full reporter pay, and it's not bad, considering our size and circulation."

"No," Amy had to agree. "It isn't." She paused for a long

214

moment. "Still . . . I don't know, Nancy. It's a great offer, but . . ."

Nancy smiled at her. "Please, give it some thought. I don't need an answer right this minute. Let me know what you decide, OK?"

Amy's answer was postponed by a young lady carrying a small tray and setting a cup of coffee in front of each of the women. She placed a tiny cream pitcher and an equally minute sugar bowl on the desk and left the office. Amy sipped her coffee, black. It was excellent.

"I'll think about it, Nancy," Amy promised, "and get back to you in a couple of days, either way."

"Good. You do that." She raised her coffee cup, drank, and said, "Enough about business. Tell me how you decided on Coldwater, and what you think of the Old West so far." The conversation shifted comfortably to other topics. They chatted until their coffee cups were empty.

"I'll let you get back to work," Amy said, standing. "Thanks for asking me in. I'll be in touch."

Nancy Lewis stood behind her desk and extended her right hand. As Amy took it, Nancy said, "My pleasure. I hope I'll be welcoming you aboard the next time we talk. If not, though, let's keep in touch."

Amy felt the barely noticeable rumble far beneath her feet as she walked back to the entrance at the *News-Express* and out onto the sidewalk. *Suppose it was one of my stories those presses were churning out?* The thought intrigued her.

There was no line at the car wash—another benefit of small-town living. Bobby went berserk as the big, soapy brushes circled the Jeep; he barked wildly and leaped in the rear area to follow their movement.

The drive home was uneventful. Amy replayed her visit with Nancy Lewis in her mind, still a tad dazed by the woman's cordiality and the offer of employment. *It's been a while—other than the Eagle Scout piece—since I've been a journalist. Fiction is my focus now, the direction of my writing. Still, there's not a thing wrong with drawing a paycheck every two weeks, and there's no reason I can't work on my novel on my own time. I don't know, though—can I produce what the* News-Express *wants day after day, story after story?* Another, stronger thought took the place of her self-doubt. *Of course I can! And as Nancy said, writing is writing, and that's what I am—a writer. I just don't know about the job right now.*

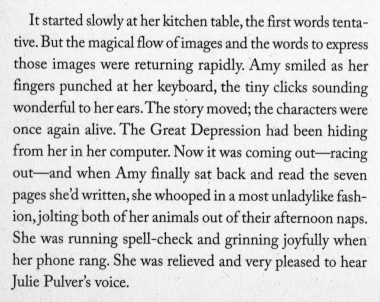

It started slowly at her kitchen table, the first words tentative. But the magical flow of images and the words to express those images were returning rapidly. Amy smiled as her fingers punched at her keyboard, the tiny clicks sounding wonderful to her ears. The story moved; the characters were once again alive. The Great Depression had been hiding from her in her computer. Now it was coming out—racing out—and when Amy finally sat back and read the seven pages she'd written, she whooped in a most unladylike fashion, jolting both of her animals out of their afternoon naps. She was running spell-check and grinning joyfully when her phone rang. She was relieved and very pleased to hear Julie Pulver's voice.

"Are you in the middle of something?" Julie asked. Her voice was breathless.

"Not really," Amy said. "What's up?"

"You have to come over here right now! OK?" There was such excitement in Julie's voice that Amy was confused. "Sure. But what's going on? You sound like a little kid on Christmas morning."

Julie laughed. "It's much, much better than that, Amy. Come on, get moving. You need to be here!" There was a sound in the background Amy couldn't quite identify. "I gotta run," Julie told her. "But hurry over here."

Amy did hurry. She clipped Bobby to his chain outside the garage, filled his water bowl, and jumped into her Jeep. As she swung out onto the road from her driveway, her tires chirped as she stepped a bit too heavily on the gas pedal. She was very curious about what had her friend so wound up, but there was no doubt that it was good news, and she smiled to herself as she drove.

Only Julie's pickup was in the driveway at the Pulver home. Danny's veterinary van was missing from its parking spot. Amy pulled behind Julie's truck and got out of her Jeep. As she started toward the front door, Julie called to her from a side window. "Come on in, Amy. I'll be with you in a minute."

Julie's living room, as Amy remembered it, was neat, orderly, and welcoming. The furniture was far from brand new, but it was of good quality, and it was comfortable, meant to be used. When she heard her friend's footsteps, she turned to find Julie standing in the doorway of the living room with a pink blanket-wrapped bundle in her arms. The smile on Julie's face was genuinely beatific.

"This is Tessa Sarah Pulver," Julie said, her words so full of love and awe. Amy moved forward to mother and child. The infant had a tangle of black hair, and her tiny hands moved as if reaching out to Amy. When Amy extended a finger, Tessa grasped it, holding it with a strength that seemed impossible for such a young baby.

"She's beautiful," Amy said.

"Tessa is what all the rush and the secrecy were about the other night," Julie explained. "Danny and I applied through an adoption service a while back, and we were told that when a baby became available, we had to be ready to move fast. We did all the paperwork—and waited and waited. When we got the call we had to race to Billings to catch a flight to New York City—and here we are."

"I'm so happy for you and Danny," Amy said. "Will Tessa call me Aunt Amy?"

"Of course she will! Let's sit down, and you can hold her while I make us some tea."

Amy was somewhat dubious about that. "I don't know. I haven't had any experience with babies."

"Neither have I," Julie said cheerfully. "And I'm doing just fine. So will you."

Tessa squirmed a bit when Julie put her into Amy's arms, but the baby settled down quickly. In moments the infant was asleep, her breathing even, her breath warm against Amy's neck. Tessa smelled of milk and baby powder and baby shampoo. Amy relaxed holding the child, wondering if she'd ever hold a baby of her own. Maternal instinct washed over her like a sudden tidal wave. *One day . . .* she thought.

Julie came back into the living room with two mugs of tea and sat next to Amy on the couch. "We didn't know when—or even if—this would happen," she explained. "We checked with agencies in the major cities, the national ones, but the fees were astronomical. Then Ian and Maggie told us about this group that places children from third world countries. We were put on the list after the agency did a home visit and reviewed our backgrounds and all that." She sighed. "We decided we wouldn't tell anyone until our baby was actually with us, because we didn't really know that it would happen. We believed it would, and we prayed about it, but we wanted to keep it to ourselves until it actually happened." She reached for Tessa. "She's zonked out. I'll put her in her crib, and then we can chat."

Within a few moments Julie returned to the living room and sat down once again next to Amy. "So," she said, "how's the novel coming?"

An equivocal "OK" almost escaped from Amy's lips—but didn't. "It's moving real well," she said.

"Good. Speaking of writing," Julie said, "the Bennett story was dynamite. Nancy loved it. I talked to her earlier, and she told me about your meeting this morning." She hesitated for a moment. "I hope you take the job—I really do. When I come back we'd be working together. Lou, the other reporter, will be retiring within a few months. But I guess you knew that." She paused again. "I think it'd be great to work with you, Amy."

"I need to—" Amy began but was interrupted by a sound that almost immediately became a howl from Tessa's room. Both women got to their feet. "I'll think about the job," Amy promised. "Go take care of your daughter. We'll talk again soon."

Amy's happiness for Julie and Danny rode with her on the way back to her home. Danny and Julie were a couple who had all the love in the world to give to each other, to animals, to their friends, and now to their child.

She sat in her Jeep in the driveway for a few minutes, knowing that there was a telephone call she owed—one she had to make, as difficult as she knew it'd be. For a moment she considered driving over there but decided against it. That'd just make things harder on both of them.

What a day, she thought as she let herself and Bobby into her house. *The meeting with Nancy Lewis, the happiness at the Pulver home.*

Amy went directly to her telephone, checked her directory, and placed the call.

"Hello, Ben Callan."

"Ben, it's Amy. Do you have a minute?"

"Sure, Amy. I, uh, was going to call you a little later. Hold on for a second, OK? I'm just about to fill Zack's water bowl, and then I'll be right with you."

Amy heard steps move away from the telephone and a door open. *Honesty is the best policy*, she assured herself. *I'll tell him about my feelings for Jake and how I find it impossible to be a part of two men's lives at the same time. I know in my heart that what I feel for Jake doesn't leave any room in my life*

220

for another guy, except as a friend. I'll tell Ben that I hope we can be friends and apologize for how things appeared at his place. If things were different . . . but they're not different. She looked down at Bobby, who was sitting at her feet with his eyes on her face, staring at her as if he expected her to explain her sudden tension. She reached down with her free hand and scratched between his ears. *If it hadn't been for Ben . . .*

"Amy? Hi. Like I said, I was going to call you." His voice sounded different to Amy—tight, somehow, as if he were about to convey bad news. She heard him take a breath. "When we were together I had some strong feelings."

"I did too, Ben. But that's why I'm calling. I'm afraid that I—"

"Wait. Please." He drew another breath. He spoke more rapidly than was normal for him. "I hadn't really spent any time with a lady since Sandy. Being with you made me . . . the thing is, I could feel interest on your part, and I really enjoyed that, and we got along so easily. I loved talking with you, and I loved looking at you too."

"Ben, there's something I need to—"

He went on as if he hadn't heard her last words. "You reminded me of how good I used to feel with Sandy. I called her after you left. I've never stopped loving her, Amy—not for a second. We talked for a long time. She's coming back for a visit here in a couple of weeks. If there's anything I can do short of moving to Chicago to get us back together, I'm going to do it." He paused for a long moment. "Us seeing one another would be unfair to you, Amy—and I won't let that happen. I hope you can understand."

Amy swallowed before answering. "I understand perfectly, Ben. You're a good man, and I appreciate your candor and your honesty. I hope for the best for you and Sandy—and I mean that."

Ben sounded tremendously relieved. "Thanks, Amy. You're a great lady. If things were different, well . . ."

"I know, Ben. But they're not." She paused. "Maybe after a while we could have coffee at the café or something. After all, Bobby and Zack are friends now. Maybe they can play together again."

"Sure," Ben said. "Let's do that."

Amy figured that Ben knew as well as she did that the meeting would never be planned, that any contact between them, at least in the near future, would be fortuitous, that they'd perhaps run into one another in town.

But it was a good way to end a conversation that was difficult for both parties.

❧

Jake's gentle tapping at the door came at about ten o'clock that night. Amy checked through the peephole—a habit she'd carried to Coldwater from her city-living years—and opened the door. She saw immediately that Jake's face was drawn and pale and that he looked terribly weary. He stepped inside wordlessly, and Amy moved to him.

"What is it, Jake? You look terrible. Did something happen?" she said, moving her face back an inch from his shoulder but not pushing back from their embrace. For a time he clung to her without speaking.

"Come on," she said quietly. "Let's sit down."

They sat very close together on the couch. Only the reading lamp was on, but there was enough light for Amy to see the pain in Jake's eyes.

"I talked to Mallory," he said. After a long pause, he continued, his voice raw with emotion, quiet, so that Amy had to strain to hear some of his words.

"I had no idea at all," he said. "Mal was another employee—like Wes or Wade or any of the guys. I like them all, and I care about them all, but I'm not really personally involved in their lives. Now I can see that some of what Mallory said and did should have alerted me to how she felt."

"Like what, Jake?"

"Well . . . no really big things, I guess. But she came by my place a bit too often, for no real reason—just to kinda visit. And she'd get sort of dressed up for no reason, just to tell me something about one of the horses she was working with." His hand found Amy's, and he clutched it, probably more strongly than he realized. "I feel like a real jerk now. But I honestly didn't know what sort of feelings she was harboring. I never led her on in any way—you have my word on that.

"I never thought of myself as being insensitive. I've helped out employees who needed a little money for an emergency, and I even bailed one of my guys out of jail after he got in a bar fight. But with Mallory . . ." He shook his head. "When she came here with her father years ago, I could see he paid next to no attention to her, and maybe I was extra nice to her because of that. But she was a grown woman—only three

223

or four years younger than I am. I didn't think in terms of romance and crushes. I thought that was high school stuff. I guess I kind of assumed she had a guy at home."

"Maybe the word *crush* is a high school thing," Amy said. "But having strong feelings for someone isn't." Her eyes found Jake's. "I'm afraid men don't always pick up on things like that. It's not that they're insensitive or uncaring, but . . . well . . . oblivious. What's blatantly obvious to a woman can pass right over a guy's head."

"I think maybe she was picking up on how I was beginning to feel about you, Amy. 'Cause I think that was fairly apparent to anyone paying any attention. That would account for the way she treated you. That I *did* see—but had no idea what to do about it. I asked her once, after the storm, and she said that I was imagining things."

Amy nodded and waited for Jake to go on. He let go of her hand and draped his arm over her shoulders.

"What did you say to her tonight?"

"I told her about us, that we loved one another. That we were going to be together. Then, I told her she'd have to leave."

Amy drew a breath that sounded much like a gasp.

"I couldn't keep her around as an employee knowing how she feels about you, and about me. It's a big ranch, but it's not big enough to hold something like that. I gave her as much of a severance package as I could. Her work with horses is great, and I'll give her a reference letter that says just that. I wished her the best, and I meant that. But she can't stay here. Maybe if she's away from me, she'll get her life together. I hope so."

"I'm sorry. All that must have been hard for you, Jake."

Jake nodded sadly. "I wish there'd been some easy way to fix all this, Amy." He was quiet for a time. "I should've seen what was happening. Maybe early on I could've changed the direction of what Mal was feeling, but I didn't see what was right in front of me. I've got to work on that, learn to be more aware of what's going on in other people's lives."

"You're not insensitive, Jake," Amy assured him. "Should you have somehow noticed what was happening with Mallory? I don't know. But I do know this: beating yourself up over it isn't going to accomplish anything for her or for you."

"I guess you're right," Jake said. He stood, and Amy stood with him. "I'm going back to my place now, get some sleep. How about if I come over in the morning and we go to the café for breakfast?"

"I'd like that."

They hugged at the door. Jake's whispered "I love you" was spoken into her hair as he held her. The words were just as precious this time as they'd been the first.

Amy was suddenly as tired as she could ever recall being. She turned off the living room lamp and slowly went up the stairs to her bedroom in the dark.

In the smallest hours of that night, not too long before dawn, Amy was stirred from sleep by the muted grumbling of a truck engine from Jake's place. She listened, half awake, for a minute, and then sleep and the dream of Jake Winter she'd been savoring claimed her once again.

In the morning Mallory's silver Airstream was gone from the place where it had rested for the past month.

10

Amy's new leather desk chair whooshed quietly as she leaned against the thick, luxurious padding of the back behind her. The chair had been a bit of an extravagance, but she was spending so much time up here in her den that the investment seemed worthwhile. And, since the money came from the advance on her second novel, she felt justified. Further, the check every two weeks from the *News-Express* made a big difference.

Snow beat against the den window, sounding like tossed sand against the glass. The wind, seeking something else to numb and freeze, whistled outside, gathering its strength for another day of subarctic, December-in-Montana temperatures. Amy looked out the window to her side and shivered as she watched the snow whirl crazily about in the open space between the house and the big steel building.

She reached down and ruffled the fur at Bobby's shoulders before she refocused on her keyboard and monitor. The collie grunted happily, shifted his position slightly, and went back to sleep. Nutsy, dozing on a prerelease copy of *The Longest Years*, didn't stir.

Amy couldn't see her old home from where her den was positioned, and she was glad of that. *It was—is—a great place. And,* she reminded herself, *the family in it now loves it—the kids have a pony and two dogs, and the garden in back that they all work on is using that land the way it should be used.* She smiled. *I didn't want Jake to see me cry the day I handed over the keys, but then I'm glad he did. Talking about it made everything better.*

Movement outside caught her attention. Wes, bundled up in a long duster with his Stetson snugged on his head with a scarf that covered his ears and tied under his chin, was carrying something big with a tarp tied over it toward the house. He leaned against gusts of wind and struggled to keep control of the awkward thing he was carrying.

She heard Wes's quiet tapping at the back door, and Jake slide his chair back from the kitchen table to tug the door open. She heard their voices—she even heard the *sshhhh* one of them warned the other with.

"Darn good thing we don't have no brass monkeys outside, Jake," Wes said. "They'd be ruined if we did."

Amy heard something clunk down on the kitchen floor. "OK if I take a look?" Jake asked.

"Nope, it ain't. Miss Amy gets the first peek. That's only right. Where's she at?"

"Upstairs," Jake said, "working on her book."

"Takes some time to write one of them things, don't it?"

"Takes as much patience as it does time," Jake said. "But she says it's coming along real well." He moved to the doorway, his boots thumping on the floor. "Amy? Can you come down here for a second?"

"Be right there. Let me shut down up here."

Amy smiled when she saw Wes standing in the kitchen. Bobby, at her heels, dashed to his friend, tail swinging, nosing at the old cowboy's pocket for the treat he knew was hidden in it.

She stopped abruptly when she noticed the sawhorse's legs revealed under the tarp. "What's this?"

"Everything happened kinda quick, and I didn't have time to get your gift ready, Miss Amy," Wes said. "I wanted you to have somethin' I made with my own hands. So, this is a combination—it's your Christmas present too. Go on, take the cover off of it."

Amy stepped to the center of the kitchen, crouched down, and began working the knot in the twine that held the tarp in place. The sharply bright winter light that streamed in the window brought glittering life to the diamond on Amy's finger and the simple gold wedding band in front of it. She whisked the tarp away and brought her hand to her mouth in awe. "Wes, it's beautiful. Thanks so much. I love it."

The Western stock saddle was a thing of beauty, yet more so because it'd been made with the skills of a man who knew and loved horses. The leather, hand-tanned and precisely cut and stitched, released its natural perfume into the room.

Montana folks, Amy had learned, weren't much for hugging, but that didn't stop her. She rushed into Wes's arms, embracing him, holding him tightly for a long moment.

"It's wonderful, Wes. I'll ride it forever and ever, and each time I step in a stirrup, I'll think of you."

Wes shifted his boots nervously a bit, suddenly unsure what to do with his hands as he stepped back from Amy. "Thing is, a good saddle don't really wear out. I thought maybe when you an' Jake start a family, a little boy might sit that saddle too." After a second he added quickly, "Or maybe a little girl, 'course."

Amy's eyes met Jake's for a moment. They both smiled. Neither had realized that Wes Newton could predict the future—the future that was less than seven months away on Amy and Jake Winter's ranch.

A Sneak Peek at

Paige Lee Elliston's Next Book,

Northern Hearts

There must be a million of these awful things!

Tessa Rollins frantically waved her gloved hands in front of the gauze veil that hung from the narrow brim of her hat and surrounded her head. *No, a billion—at least a billion. And they lurk around out here, waiting for me.*

The cloud of Alaskan black flies *was* a cloud, a thick, turgid, slow-moving mass that blotted out the bright sunlight and ebbed and flowed around Tessa's shrouded face. The swirling horde of insects emitted a frantic buzzing sound that was unlike anything she'd ever heard before.

"Put them good thick rubber bands around your pant cuffs and your sleeves, or the flies, they'll crawl right on up your legs an' arms, and I'll tell you what—when they take a bite outta you, it feels like someone dripped molten metal right on your skin," the elderly woman at the Denali Park Service office had told her. "Some folks, they put wads of cotton soaked in linseed oil in their ears and noses. See, the flies go on into wherever its warm and dark to lay their eggs . . . Thing is, they're really not too bad, 'cept for a couple, maybe three weeks every year. Ya know? When they're bad, though, you might want to keep your face covered much as you can."

Of course, I first set foot in Alaska just in time for prime mosquito season—and these things make the mosquitoes seem like tiny bluebirds of happiness.

Tessa stumbled and lurched to where her university-provided Jeep was parked, her vision, already impeded by the gauze, even less clear because of the fog of insects around her. *For this I left Clearwater, Minnesota? To be carried off by a mass of scary and disgusting bugs? I'm living in a one-room cabin with electricity that works part time, a rotary dial telephone that ends conversations whenever it wants to. I must be totally crazy.* She clambered into the vehicle and slammed the door.

Then, she took in her surroundings through the scratched and slightly glazed windows, and that made all the difference. *It's a silly cliché, but Alaska takes my breath away. The vastness, the wonderful, untouched purity of it—the exuberance of the land, the sky, the air, the people. I've never seen anything like it.*

The ancient Jeep was the boxcar-sized model, a Cherokee. When the odometer stopped working long before Tessa was given the keys, it had read over three hundred thousand miles. Regardless of its age and its battered appearance, the Jeep ran well; the powerful V8 engine purred, and the windows were blessedly tight, which kept the black flies and other insects outside, where they beat against the glass as if in mindless frustration. Tessa tugged off her hat and its gauze and, completely realizing how childish it was, stuck her tongue out at the buzzing mass outside. She swept her fingers through her shoulder-length dirty-blonde hair, turned the key in the ignition, and clicked on the radio. Alaskans, she'd learned, lived by their radios and were never far from them. It wasn't that they were enchanted by the vapid mumbling of the local host or the droning Welkian music he favored. Rather, they were well aware that the Denali National Park Information Service broke into the commercial broadcasts frequently with weather advisories that could be important—not only as to potential storms but to planned events that Alaskans seemed to love so much, and even to the planting of backyard crops.

The Park, as the natives called it, as if there were no other national parks on the planet, encompassed 6 million acres of the largest state in the union, more than 7,300 square miles of the wildest, most unpredictable, most unforgiving, and essentially unexplored wilderness frontiers on earth. Tessa, after slightly less than three months in-country—the native term—still couldn't find the right words to describe Alaska when she wrote home. *Majestic, awe-inspiring, pristine, infinitely beautiful*, all sounded bland to her—like describing the Atlantic Ocean as *sizable* and *damp*.

The Jeep's knobby, heavy-duty tires thumped and crunched confidently over the ruts and pits of the access road that led to Tessa's cabin. As soon as the snow started, she'd have to leave her vehicle in a three-sided shelter just off the main highway to Fairview and use the old Ski-Doo provided to her as part of her job benefits to get back and forth from her home to the road. She hadn't yet experienced a winter in Alaska, but she'd spent most of her life in Minnesota, where she'd been born, educated, and until recently had taught anthropology at the same university where she'd taken her undergrad and graduate degrees. She believed she'd seen pretty much the worst of weather. The fact that the Inuits had forty-six different words for snow bothered her a tad. *Still*, she thought, *snow is snow and cold is cold, whether it's in Minnesota or Alaska.*

The last pile of clippings from newspapers, magazines, and newsletters her administrators at the university had mailed to her shifted forward on the passenger seat as Tessa braked for a cow moose standing in the road fifty yards ahead. The massive animal watched the oncoming vehicle for several moments and then swung her huge head away, apparently more interested in something at the roadside. Tessa tapped her horn. The moose paid no attention. Tessa downshifted, drifted to a stop, and hit her horn again, this time a bit longer. The moose favored Tessa with another glance, her barrel-sized ribcage expanded with a deep breath that it released in a moment, as if sighing, and rather disdainfully strolled into the thick woods on the other side of the road. The sheer size of a moose had astounded Tessa the first time she'd seen one in the wild, and still did each time she came across one. The first was an adult male whose span from the left tip to the right of his rack was every bit of six and a half feet. At home a friend of her father's raised Clydesdales, and she knew that a 1,400-pound draft horse wasn't uncommon. That bull moose she gauged to weigh perhaps 1,800 pounds since he stood a good seven feet tall at his shoulder.

Tessa wished she could change her perception of moose

in general. *I know it's unfair, but they seem to be . . . well . . . dumb creatures, lumbering around as if they're in some sort of a daze, wandering through settlements and towns like they're alone in the world, chomping mouthfuls of leaves, twigs, and weeds . . .*

She grinned at the cow as it ambled off. "There ya go, ma'am—queen of all you survey," she said aloud to the departing moose's massive rear quarters.

The road was clear in both directions, as it almost always was. Tessa still marveled at the absence of traffic, the lack of city sounds, that was so much a part of life in the vast reaches of her new state. She marveled in the same manner too at the string of coincidences and happenstance situations that had brought her here.

At thirty-six and on a tenure path in the department of anthropology at the university, Tessa had fallen into a disquieting monotony in her life. Days were essentially the same; semesters flowed into one another with little to differentiate one from those it followed. Her students became almost faceless, her social life bland but not actually unpleasant. She was alone but not often lonely. Still, she felt a sort of general emptiness. She didn't believe that she was meant to live her life alone, without a loving partner, but the men she dated—other professionals and academics—didn't trip the chord in her heart that she genuinely believed she'd feel when the right man came into her life.

When the chair of the anthropology department had called her to his office six months ago, Tessa had been both surprised and curious. In his somewhat wordy and more than a little pompous fashion, Dr. Turner had told Tessa that he'd seen her article. She'd written the piece for an anthropology journal on the effects of the twenty-first century on closed cultures, those largely untouched by the modern world. As an example, she'd cited a tribe in the jungles of Borneo whose members, after sighting their first airplane in the sky, began to worship it as a god, to offer sacrifices to it, to eventually attribute to it sweeping powers over all aspects of their lives from fertility to death to changes in the weather. That, Turner told her, brought to mind his correspondence with an anthropologist colleague in Alaska who'd been studying a small group of Inuit people living on the outskirts of Denali National Park. Their way of life had been unchanged for hundreds of generations but was now in many ways in conflict with the encroachment of modernity. It'd be interesting, Turner thought, to "look into it."

Then he'd laid out the string of coincidences to her. The colleague had seen Tessa's article and compared what she wrote to his study in Alaska. The daughter of that anthropologist's sister's minister had taken courses under Tessa and was impressed with her, and that had somehow gotten back to the colleague. He was about to retire and, as an old fraternity pal of Turner's, contacted Turner about Tessa Rollins—and the offer of an open-ended study of at least one year in Alaska was ultimately made to her.